Susan Warner

Karl Krinken

His Christmas stocking

Susan Warner

Karl Krinken
His Christmas stocking

ISBN/EAN: 9783337384418

Printed in Europe, USA, Canada, Australia, Japan

Cover: Foto ©Andreas Hilbeck / pixelio.de

More available books at **www.hansebooks.com**

KARL KRINKEN,

HIS CHRISTMAS STOCKING.

BY THE AUTHORS OF

"*THE WIDE, WIDE WORLD*," "*QUEECHY*,"
"*DIANA*," ETC. ETC.

LONDON:

JAMES NISBET & CO., 21 BERNERS STREET.

MDCCCLXXVIII.

SUGGESTIVE.

I THINK it necessary to come to the help of the Public—

Lest Miss Wetherell should not have her dues, they are giving her the dues of every one else; and whatever my hand may have to do on " Ellen Montgomery's Bookshelf," there it is — even though " a discerning Public" perceive it not. No matter for that—I had as lief be behind the books as before them; but must enter my protest against facts which are no facts.

Therefore kind Public, Messrs Editors, and friends in general, I propose this division of the volumes; by which my sister and I will each in turn have written them all. *Whatever book or part of a book you particularly like, thank Miss Wetherell for it;* and let all those pages which are less interesting be charged to the account of

AMY LOTHROP.

New York. Dec. 13. 1853.

CONTENTS.

THE CHRISTMAS STOCKING.

WHEREVER Santa Claus lives, and in whatever spot of the universe he harnesses his reindeer and loads up his sleigh, one thing is certain—he never yet put anything in that sleigh for little Carl Krinken. Indeed it may be noted as a fact, that the Christmas of poor children has but little of his care. Now and then a cast-off frock or an extra mince pie slips into the load, as it were accidentally; but in general Santa Claus strikes at higher game,—gilt books, and sugar-plums, and fur tippets, and new hoods, and crying babies, and rocking-horses, and guns, and drums, and trumpets;—and what have poor children to do with these? Not but they might have something to do with them. It is a singular fact that poor children cut their teeth quite as early as the rich.

B

—even that sweet tooth, which is destined to be an unsatisfied tooth all the days of its life, unless its owner should perchance grow up to be a sugar-refiner. It is also remarkable, that though poor children can bear a great deal of cold, they can also enjoy being warm—whether by means of a new dress or a load of firing; and the glow of a bright blaze looks just as comfortable upon little cheeks that are generally blue, as upon little cheeks that are generally red; while not even dirt will hinder the kindly heat of a bed of coals from rejoicing little shivering fingers that are held over it.

I say all this is strange—for nobody knows much about it; and how can they? When a little girl once went down Broadway with her muff and her doll, the hand outside the muff told the hand within that he had no idea what a cold day it was. And the hand inside said that for his part he never wished it to be warmer.

But with all this Santa Claus never troubled his head—he was too full of business, and wrapped up in buffalo skins besides; and though he sometimes thought of little Carl, as a good-natured little fellow who talked as much about *him* as if Santa Claus had given him half the world—yet it ended with a thought. for his hands were indeed well occupied. It was no trifle to fill half a million of *rich* little stockings; and then—how many poor children had any to fill? or if one chanced to be found, it might have holes in it; and if the sugar-plums came rolling down upon such a floor—— !

To be sure the children wouldn't mind that, but Santa Claus would.

Nevertheless, little Carl always hung up his stocking, and generally had it filled—though not from any sleigh-load of wonderful things; and he often amused himself Christmas eve with dreaming that he had made himself sick eating candy, and that they had a stack of mince-pies as high as the house. So altogether, what with dreams and realities, Carl enjoyed that time of year very much, and thought it was a great pity Christmas did not come every day. He was always contented, too, with what he found in his stocking; while some of his rich little neighbours had theirs filled only to their heart's *dis*content, and fretted because they had what they did, or because they hadn't what they didn't have. It was a woful thing if a top was painted the wrong colour, or if the mane of a rocking-horse was too short, or if his bridle was black leather instead of red.

But when Carl once found in his stocking a little board nailed upon four spools for wheels, and with no better tongue than a long piece of twine, *his* little tongue ran as fast as the spools, and he had brought his mother a very small load of chips in less than five minutes. And a small cake of maple-sugar, which somehow once found its way to the same depending toe, was a treasure quite too great to be weighed : though it measured only an inch and a half across, and though the maple-trees had grown about a foot since it was made.

" Wife," said John Krinken, " what shall we put in little Carl's stocking to-night?"

" Truly," said his wife. " I do not know. Nevertheless we must find something, though there be but little in the house."

And the wind swept round and round the old hut, and every cupboard-door rattled and said in an empty sort of way, " There is not much here."

John Krinken and his wife lived on the coast, where they could hear every winter storm rage and beat, and where the wild sea sometimes brought wood for them and laid it at their very door. It was a drift-wood fire by which they sat now, this Christmas eve,—the crooked knee of some ship, and a bit of her keel, with nails and spikes rust-held in their places, and a piece of green board stuck under to light the whole. The andirons were two round stones, and the hearth was a flat one ; and in front of the fire sat John Krinken on an old box making a fish-net, while a splinter chair upheld Mrs. Krinken and a half-mended red flannel shirt. An old chest between the two held patches and balls of twine ; and the crooked knee, the keel, and the green board, were their only candles.

"We must find something," repeated John. And pausing with his netting-needle half through the loop, he looked round towards one corner of the hut.

A clean rosy little face and a very complete set of thick curls rested there, in the very middle of the thin pillow and the hard bed ; while the coverlet of blue check was tucked round and in, lest the drift-wood fire should not do its duty at that distance.

John Krinken and his wife refreshed them-selves with a long look, and then returned to their work.

" You've got the stocking, wife ?" said John, after a pause

"Ay," said his wife: "it's easy to find something to fill it."

"Fetch it out, then, and let's see how much 'twill take to fill it."

Mrs. Krinken arose, and going to one of the two little cupboards she brought thence a large iron key; and then having placed the patches and thread upon the floor, she opened the chest, and rummaged out a long grey woollen stocking, with white toe and heel and various darns in red. Then she locked the chest again and sat down as before.

"The same old thing," said John Krinken with a glance at the stocking.

"Well," said his wife, "it's the only stocking in the house that's long enough."

"I know one thing he shall have in it," said John; and he got up and went to the other cupboard, and fetched from it a large piece of cork.

"He shall have a boat that will float like one of Mother Carey's chickens." And he began to cut and shape with his large clasp-knife, while the little heap of chips on the floor between his feet grew larger, and the cork grew more and more like a boat.

His wife laid down her hand which was in the sleeve of the red jacket, and watched him.

" It 'll never do to put that in first," she said ; " the masts would be broke. I guess I'll fill the toe of the stocking with apples."

" And where will you get apples?" said John Krinken, shaping the keel of his boat.

" I've got 'em," said his wife,—" three rosy-cheeked apples. Last Saturday, as I came from market, a man went by with a load of apples ; and as I came on I found that he had spilled three out of his wagon. So I picked them up."

" Three apples—" said John. " Well, I'll give him a red cent to fill up the chinks."

" And I've got an old purse that he can keep it in," said the mother.

" How long do you suppose he'll keep it?" said John.

" Well, he'll want to put it somewhere while he does keep it," said Mrs. Krinken. " The purse is old, but it was handsome once ; and it'll please the child any way. And then there's his new shoes."

So when the boat was done Mrs. Krinken brought out the apples and slipped them into the stocking; and then the shoes went in, and the purse, and the red cent—which of course ran all the way down to the biggest red darn of all, in the very toe of the stocking.

But there was still abundance of room left.

"If one only had some sugar things," said Mrs. Krinken.

"Or some nuts," said John.

"Or a book," rejoined his wife. "Carl takes to his book, wonderfully."

"Yes," said John, "all three would fill up in fine style. Well, there is a book he can have— only I don't know what it is, nor whether he'd like it. That poor lady we took from an American wreck when I was mate of the Skeen-elf—it had lain in her pocket all the while, and she gave it to me when she died—because I didn't let her die in the water, poor soul! She said it was worth a great deal. And I guess the clasp is silver."

"O I dare say he'd like it," said Mrs. Krinken. "Give him that, and I'll put in the old pine-cone,—he's old enough to take care of it now. I guess he'll be content."

The book with its brown leather binding and tarnished silver clasp was dusted and rubbed up and put in, and the old sharp-pointed pine cone followed; and the fisherman and his wife followed it up with a great deal of love and a blessing.

And then the stocking was quite full.

It was midnight; and the fire had long been covered up, and John Krinken and his wife were fast asleep, and little Carl was in the midst of the hard bed and his sweet dreams as before. The stocking hung by the side of the fire-place, as still as if it had never walked about in its life, and not a sound could be heard but the beat of the surf upon the shore and an occasional sigh from the wind; for the wind is always melancholy at Christmas.

Once or twice an old rat had peeped cautiously out of his hole, and seeing nobody, had crossed the floor and sat down in front of the stocking, which his sharp nose immediately pointed out to him. But though he could smell the apples plain enough, he was afraid that long thing might hold a trap as well; and so he did nothing but smell and snuff and show his teeth. As for the little mice, they ran out and danced a measure on the hearth and then back again; after which one of them squealed for some time for the amusement of the rest.

But just at midnight there was another noise heard — as somebody says;

> " You could hear on the roof
> The scraping and prancing of each little hoof,"—

and down came Santa Claus through the chimney

He must have set out very early that night, to have so much time to spare, or perhaps he was cold in spite of his furs: for he came empty-handed, and had evidently no business calls in that direction. But the first thing he did was to examine the stocking and its contents.

At some of the articles he laughed, and at some he frowned, but most of all did he shake his head over the love that filled up all the spare room in the stocking. It was a kind of thing Santa Claus wasn't used to; the little stockings were generally too full for anything of that sort,—when they had to hold candy enough to make the child sick, and toys enough to make him unhappy because he didn't know which to play with first, of course very little love could get in. And there is no telling how many children would be satisfied if it did. But Santa Claus put all the things back just as he had found them, and stood smiling to himself for a minute, with his hands on his sides and his back to the fire. Then tapping the stocking with a little stick that he carried, he bent down over Carl and whispered some words in his ear, and went off up the chimney.

And the little mice came out and danced on the floor till the day broke.

" Christmas day in the morning ! " And what

a day it was! All night long as the hours went by, the waves had beat time with their heavy feet; and wherever the foam and spray had fallen, upon board or stone or crooked stick, there it had frozen, in long icicles or fringes or little white caps. But when the sun had climbed out of the leaden sea, every bit of foam and ice sparkled and twinkled like morning stars, and the Day got her cheeks warm and glowing just as fast as she could; and the next thing the sun did was to walk in at the hut window and look at little Carl Krinken. Then it laid a warm hand upon his little face, and Carl had hardly smiled away the last bit of his dream before he started up in his bed and shouted

" Merry Christmas! "

The mice were a good deal startled, for they had not all seen their partners home; but they got out of the way as fast as they could, and when Carl bounded out of bed he stood alone upon the floor.

The floor felt cold—very. Carl's toes curled up in the most disapproving manner possible, and he tried standing on his heels. Then he scampered across the floor, and began to feel of the stocking — beginning at the top. It was plain enough what the shoes were, but the other things puzzled him till he got to the foot of the stocking; and *his* feet being by that time very cold (for both toes and heels had rested on the floor in the eagerness of examination), Carl seized the stocking in both hands and scampered back to bed again; screaming out,

"Apples! apples! apples!"

His mother being now nicely awaked by his clambering over her for the second time, she gave him a kiss and a "Merry Christmas," and got up; and as his father did the same, Carl was left in undisturbed possession of the warm bed. There he laid himself down as snug as could be, with the long stocking by his side, and began to pull out and examine the things one by one,—after which each article was laid on the counterpane outside.

"Well little boy, how do you like your things?" said Mrs. Krinken, coming up to the bed just when Carl and the empty stocking lay side by side.

"Firstrate!" said Carl. "Mother, I dreamed last night that all my presents told me stories. Wasn't it funny?"

"Yes, I suppose so," said his mother, as she walked away to turn the fish that was broiling. Carl lay still and looked at the stocking.

" Where did you come from, old stocking ? ".
said he.

" From England," said the stocking, very
softly.

Carl started right up in bed, and looked between
the sheets, and over the counterpane, and behind
the head-board—there was nothing to be seen.
Then he shook the stocking as hard as he could,
but something in it struck his other hand pretty
hard too. Carl laid it down and looked at it
again, and then cautiously putting in his hand,
he with some difficulty found his way to the
very toe,—there lay the red cent, just where
it had been all the time, upon the biggest of the
red darns

" A red cent!" cried Carl. " O I guess it
was you talking, wasn't it?"

" No," said the red cent. " But I can
talk."

" Do you know where you came from?" said
Carl, staring at the red cent with all his eyes.

" Certainly," said the cent.

" I dreamed that everything in my stocking
told me a story," said Carl.

" So we will," said the red cent. " Only to
you. To nobody else."

Carl shook his head very gravely, and having

slipped the red cent into the little old purse, he put everything into the stocking again and jumped out of bed. For the drift-wood fire was blazing up to the very top of the little fire-place, and breakfast was almost ready upon the old chest.

But as soon as breakfast was over, Carl carried the stocking to one corner of the hut where stood another old chest; and laying out all his treasures thereon, he knelt down before it.

" Now begin," he said. " But you mustn't all talk at once. I guess I'll hear the apples first, because I might want to eat 'em up. I don't care which of *them* begins."

THE STORY OF THE THREE APPLES.

" I assume to myself the task of relating our joint history," said the largest of the three apples, " because I am perhaps the fairest minded of us all. The judgment and experience of my younger sister, Half-ripe, are as yet immature ; and my little brother Knerly is unfortunately of a somewhat sour disposition, and therefore less likely to represent things in a pleasant light. My own name is Beachamwell."

At this opening the two smaller apples rolled over in an uncomfortable sort of way, but said nothing.

" As for me," continued Beachamwell, " I have not only been favoured with a southern exposure, but I have also made the most of whatever good influences were within my reach ; and have endeavoured to perfect myself in every quality that an apple should have. You perceive not only the fine rounding of my shape, but also the perfect and equal colour of my cheeks. My stem is smooth and erect, and my eye precisely in a line with it; and if I could be cut open this minute I should be found true to my heart's core. I am also of a very tender disposition, being what is usually called *thin-skinned;* and a very slight thing would make a permanent and deep impression. My behaviour towards every one has always been marked by the most perfect smoothness, and on intimate acquaintance I should be found remarkably sweet and pleasant."

" You'd better not say any more about yourself at present, Beachamwell," said Carl, " because I might eat you up before you got through your story, and that would be bad. Let's hear about Half-ripe and Knerly."

' My sister Half-ripe," said Beachamwell, " though with the same natural capabilities as myself, has failed to improve them. Instead of coming out into the warm and improving society of the sun and the wind, she has always preferred to meditate under the shade of a bunch of leaves; and though in part she could not help doing credit to her family, you will perceive that her time has been but half improved,—it is only one of her cheeks that has the least proper colour, while the other displays the true pale green tint of secluded study; and even the seeds of influence and usefulness within her are but half matured; but mine will be found as dark as ——"

" As the chimney-back?" suggested Carl.

" They are not exactly that colour," replied Beachamwell,—" being in fact more like mahogany."

" Well I never saw any of that," said Carl, " so you don't tell me much. Never mind, I shall know when I cut you up. Now be quick and tell about Knerly; and then give me all the history of your great, great, great grandfather apple."

" Knerly," said Beachamwell, " was a little cross-grained from the very bud. Before he had cast off the light pink dress which as you know we apples wear in our extreme youth, the dark spot might be seen. It is probable that some poisonous sting had pierced him in that tender period of his life, and the consequence is, as I have said, some hardness of heart and sourness of disposition. As you see, he has not softened under the sun's influence, though exposed to it all his life; and it is doubtful whether he ever attains a particle of the true Beachamwell colour.

There are however good spots in Knerly; and even Half-ripe can be sweet if you only get the right side of her."

" I'll be sure to do that," said Carl, " for I'll go all round. Come, go on."

" Unfortunately," said Beachamwell, " I cannot give the information which you desire about my respected and venerable ancestors. The pedigree of apples is not always well preserved, and in general the most we can boast of is the family name : nor is that often obtained except by engrafting upon a very different stock. For one generation back, however, we may claim to be true Beachamwells. From root to twig the parent tree was the right stuff. The remarkable way in which this came about I am happily able to tell you.

" A number of years ago, one Thanksgiving-eve, Widow Penly was washing up the tea-things, and her little boy Mark sat looking at her.

" ' I wish we could keep Thanksgiving, mother,' said he.

" ' Why so we will,' said his mother.

" ' But how ? ' said Mark, with a very brightened face. ' What will you do, mother ? '

" ' I'll make you some pies—if I can get anything to make them of,' said Mrs. Penly

" ' Ah but you can't,' said Mark, his countenance falling again: ' there aren't even any potatoes in the house. You used to make potato pies, didn't you, mother, when father forgot to bring home the pumpkin?'

" ' Yes,' said Mrs. Penly, but as if she scarce heard him; for other Thanksgiving-days were sweeping across the stage, where Memory's troupe was just then performing.

" ' So what will you do, mother?' repeated little Mark, when he had watched her again for a few minutes.

" ' Do?' said the widow, rousing herself. ' Why my dear if we cannot make any pies we will keep Thanksgiving without them.'

" ' I don't think one can keep Thanksgiving without *anything*,' said Mark, a little fretfully.

" ' Oh no,' said his mother, ' neither do I; but we will think about it, dear, and do the best we can. And now you may read to me while I mend this hole in your stocking. Read the hundred and third Psalm.'

" So Mark got his little Bible and began to read,—

" ' *Bless the Lord, O my soul, and forget not all his benefits: who forgiveth all thine iniquities; who healeth all thι diseases; who redeemeth thy life from destruction; who crowneth thee with lovingkindness and tender mercies ——*'

' Don't you think, Mark,' said his mother, ' that we could keep Thanksgiving for at least *one* day with only such blessings as these ? '

" ' Why yes,' said Mark, ' I suppose we could, mother—though I wasn't thinking of that.'

" ' No, of course not,' said his mother ; ' and that is the very reason why we so often long for earthly things : we are not thinking of the heavenly blessings that God has showered upon us.'

" ' But mother,' said Mark, not quite satisfied, ' it goes on to say,—

" ' *Who satisfieth thy mouth with good things ; so that thy youth is renewed like the eagle's.*'

" And Mark looked up as if he thought his mother must be posed now, if she never was before.

" It did occur to Mrs. Penly as she glanced at the child, that his cheeks were not very fat nor his dress very thick ; and that a greater plenty of pies and other relishable things might exert a happy influence upon his complexion : but she stilled her heart with that word,—

" ' *Your Father knoweth that ye have need of such things.*

" ' I am sure we have a great many good things, Mark,' she answered cheerfully,—' don't you remember that barrel of flour that came the other day? and the molasses, and the pickles? We *must* have as much as is good for us, or God would give us more; for it says in another part of that Psalm, ' *Like as a father pitieth his children, so the Lord pitieth them that fear him.*' I wouldn't keep from you anything that I thought good for you.'

" ' But you are my *mother*,' said Mark satisfactorily.

" ' Well,' said the widow, ' the Bible says that a mother may forget her child, yet will not God forget his children. So you see, dear, that if we have not a great many things which some other people have, it is not because God has forgotten to care for us, but because we are better without them.'

" 'I wonder why,' said Mark. ' Why should they hurt us any more than other people?'

" ' God knows,' said his mother. ' It is so pleasant to have him choose and direct all for us. If I could have my way, I dare say I should wish for something that would do me harm—just as you wanted to eat blackberries last summer when you were sick.'

" ' But we are not sick,' said Mark.

" ' Yes we are—sick with sin ; and sin-sick people must not have all that their sinful hearts desire ; and people who love earth too well must want some of the good things of this world, that they may think more of heaven.'

" ' Well,' said Mark, the last thing before he got into bed, ' we'll keep Thanksgiving, mother —you and I ; and we'll try to be as happy as we can without pies.'

" ' Maybe we shall have some pleasant thing that we do not think of,' said his mother, as she tucked the clothes down about him.

" ' Why what?' said Mark starting up in an instant. ' Where *could* anything come from, mother ?'

" ' From God in the first place,' she answered ; ' and he can always find a way.'

" ' Mother !' said Mark, ' there's a *great many* apples in the road by Mr. Crab's orchard.'

" ' Well, dear'—said his mother—' they don't belong to us.'

" ' But they're in the *road,*' said Mark ; ' and Mr. Smith's pigs are there all day long eating 'em.'

" ' We won't help the pigs,' said his mother smiling. ' They don't know any better, but we do. I have cause enough for thanksgiving,

Marky, in a dear little boy who always minds
what I say.'

"Mark hugged his mother very tight round the
neck, and then went immediately to sleep, and
dreamed that he was running up hill after a
pumpkin.

"But Mark woke up in the morning empty-
handed. There were plenty of sunbeams on the
bed, and though it was so late in November, the
birds sang outside the window as if they had a
great many concerts to give before winter, and
.must make haste.

"Mark turned over on his back to have both ears
free, and then he could hear his mother and the
broom stepping up and down the kitchen; and as
she swept she sang.

' Rejoice, the Lord is King;
     Your Lord and King adore:
   Mortals, give thanks and sing,
     And triumph evermore.
 Lift up your hearts, lift up your voice
 Rejoice, again I say, rejoice.

     Rejoice in glorious hope,
       Jesus the Judge shall come,
     And take his servants up
       To their eternal home;
   We soon shall hear th' archangel's voice:
   The trump of God shall sound—Rejoice!'

" Mark listened awhile till he heard his mother stop sweeping and begin to step in and out of the pantry. She wasn't setting the table, he knew, for that was always his work, and he began to wonder what they were going to have for breakfast. Then somebody knocked at the door.

" ' Here's a quart of milk, Mis' Penly,' said a voice. ' Mother guessed she wouldn't churn again 'fore next week, so she could spare it as well as not.'

" Mark waited to hear his mother pay her thanks and shut the door, and having meanwhile got into his trousers, he rushed out into the kitchen.

" ' Is it a *whole* quart, mother?'

" ' A whole quart of new milk, Mark. Isn't that good?'

" ' Delicious!' said Mark. ' I should like to drink it all up, straight. I don't mean that I should like to really, mother, only on some accounts, you know.'

" ' Well now what shall we do with it?' said his mother. ' You shall dispose of it all.'

" ' If we had some eggs we'd have a pudding,' said Mark,—' a plum-pudding. You can't make it without eggs, can you mother?'

" ' Not very well,' said Mrs. Penly. ' Nor without plums.

" ' No, so that won't do,' said Mark. ' Seems to me we could have made more use of it if it had been apples.'

" ' Ah, you are a discontented little boy,' said his mother smiling. ' Last night you would have been glad of *anything*. Now I advise that you drink a tumblerful of milk for your breakfast—'

" ' A whole tumblerful!' interrupted Mark.

" ' Yes, and another for your tea; and then you will have two left for breakfast and tea to-morrow.'

" ' But then you won't have any of it,' said Mark.

" ' I don't want any.'

" ' But you *must* have it,' said Mark. ' Now I'll tell you, mother. I'll drink a tumblerful this morning, and you shall put some in your tea; and to-night I'll drink some more, and you'll have cream, real cream; and what's left I'll drink to-morrow.'

" ' Very well,' said his mother. ' But now you must run and get washed and dressed, for breakfast is almost ready. I have made you a little shortcake, and it's baking away at a great rate in the spider.'

" ' What's shortcake made of?' said Mark, stopping with the door in his hand.

" ' This is made of flour and water, because I had nothing else.'

" ' Well don't you set the table,' said Mark, ' because I'll be back directly; and then I can talk to you about the milk while I'm putting on your cup and my tumbler and the plates.'

" It would be hard to tell how much Mark enjoyed his tumbler of milk,—how slowly he drank it—how careful he was not to leave one drop in the tumbler; while his interest in the dish of milk in the closet was quite as deep. Jack did not go oftener to see how his bean grew, than did Mark to see how his cream rose.

" Then he set out to go with his mother to church.

" The influence of the dish of milk was not quite so strong when he was out of the house,—so many things spoke of other people's dinners that Mark half forgot his own breakfast. He thought he never had seen so many apple-trees, nor so many geese and turkeys, nor so many pumpkins, as in that one little walk to church. Again and again he looked up at his mother to ask her sympathy for a little boy who had no apples, nor geese, nor pumpkin pies; but something in the sweet quiet of her face made him think of the psalm he had read last night, and Mark was silent. But after a while his mother spoke.

" ' There was once a man, Mark, who had two springs of water near his dwelling. And the furthest off was always full, but the near one sometimes ran dry. He could always fetch as much as he wanted from the further one, and the water was by far the sweetest: moreover he could if he chose draw out the water of the upper spring in such abundance that the dryness of the lower should not be noticed.'

" ' Were they pretty springs?' said Mark.

" ' The lower one was very pretty,' replied his mother, ' only the sunbeams sometimes made it too warm, and sometimes an evil-disposed person would step in and muddy it; or a cloudy sky made it look very dark. Also the flowers which grew by its side could not bear the frost. But when the sun shone just right, it was beautiful.'

" ' I don't wonder he was sorry to have it dry up, then,' said Mark.

" ' No, it was very natural; though if one drank too much of the water it was apt to make him sick. But the other spring ——' and the widow paused, while her cheek flushed and on her lips weeping and rejoicing were strangely mingled.

" ' There was ' a great Rock,' and from this ' the cold flowing waters' came in a bright stream that you could rather hear than see; yet was the

cup always filled to the very brim if it was held
there in patient trust, and no one ever knew that
spring to fail,—yea in the great droughts it was
fullest. And the water was life-giving.

" ' But this man often preferred the lower spring,
and would neglect the other when this was full ;
and if forced to seek the Rock, he was often weary
of waiting for his cup to fill, and so drew it away
with but a few drops. And he never learned to
love the upper spring as he ought, until one year
when the very grass by the lower spring was
parched, and he fled for his life to the other.
And then it happened, Mark,' said his mother
looking down at him with her eyes full of tears,
' that when the water at last began slowly to come
into the lower spring, though it was very lovely
and sweet and pleasant it never could be loved
best again.'

" ' Mother,' said Mark, ' I don't know *exactly*
what you mean, and I do know a little, too.'

" ' Why my dear,' said his mother, ' I mean
that when we lack anything this world can give,
we must fetch the more from heaven.'

" ' You love heaven very much, don't you
mother?' said Mark, looking up at her quite
wonderingly.

" ' More than you love me.'

" Mark thought that was hardly possible ; but he didn't like to contradict his mother, and besides they were now at the church-door, and had to go right in and take their seats.   Mark thought the clergyman chose the strangest text that could be for Thanksgiving-day,—it was this,—

" ' *There is nothing at all, beside this manna, before our eyes.*'

" When church was over, and Mark and his mother were walking home again, they were overtaken by little Tom Crab.

" ' Come,' said little Tom—' let's go sit on the fence and eat apples.   We sha'n't have dinner to-day till ever so late, 'cause it takes so long to get it ready ; and I'm *so* hungry.   What are you going to have for dinner ? '

" ' I don't know,' said Mark.

" ' I know what we're going to have,' said Tom, ' only I can't remember everything.   It makes me worse than ever to think of it.   Come—let's go eat apples.'

" ' I haven't got any,' said Mark.

" ' Haven't got any ! ' said Tom, letting go of Mark's elbow and staring at him—for the idea of a boy without apples had never before occurred to any of Mr. Crab's family.   ' O you mean you've eaten up all you had in your pocket ? '

" ' No,' said Mark, ' we haven't had any this
year. Last year Mr. Smith gave us a basket-
ful.'

" ' Well come along and I'll give you some,'
said Tom. ' I've got six, and I guess three'll do
me till dinner. O Mark! you ought to see the
goose roasting in our kitchen! I'll tell you what
—I guess I may as well give you the whole six,
'cause I can run home and get some more; and I
might as well be home, too, for they might have
dinner earlier than they meant to."

" And filling Mark's pockets out of his own,
Tom ran off.

" It so happened," said Beachamwell turning
herself round with a tired air when she got to
this point in her story—" it so happened, that
Mark having stopped so long to talk with Tommy
Crab, did not get home till his mother had her
things' off and the tablecloth on; and then being
in a great hurry to help her, and a rather heed-
less little boy besides; there being moreover but
one table in the room, Mark laid his six apples
upon the sill of the window which was open.
For it was a soft autumn day—the birds giving
another concert in the still air, and the sunshine
lying warm and bright upon everything. The
apples looked quite brilliant as they lay in the

window, and as Mark eat his queer little Thanksgiving dinner of bread and a bit of corned beef,
he looked at them from time to time with great
pleasure.

"But when it was almost time for the apples to
come on table ás dessert, Mark suddenly cried
out,

"'Mother! where are my six apples?'

"'Why on the window-sill,' said his mother.

"'There arcn't but five! there aren't but five!'
said Mark. 'I must have lost one coming
home!—no I didn't either.' And running to
the window, Mark looked out. There lay the
sixth apple on the ground, appropriated as the
Thanksgiving dinner of his mother's two
chickens.

"Mark could hardly keep from crying.

"'It's *too* bad!' he said—'when I hadn't but
just six! The ugly things!'

"'You called them beauties this morning,' said
his mother.

"'But just see my apple!' said Mark—'all
dirty and pecked to pieces.'

"'And just see my little boy,' said his mother—
'all red and angry. Did you suppose, my dear,
that if apples rolled off the window-sill they would
certainly fall inside?'

" ' I guess I'll never put anything there any more,' said Mark, gathering up the five apples in his arms and letting them all fall again. But they fell inside this time, and rolled over the floor.

" ' You had better decide how many apples you will eat just now,' said Mrs. Penly, ' and then put the others away in the closet.'

" ' It's too bad !' said Mark. ' I hadn't but six. And I thought you would have three and I'd have three.'

" ' Well you may have five,' said his mother smiling—' the chickens have got my part. And maybe some good will come of that yet, if it only teaches you to be careful.'

. " Oddly enough," said Beachamwell, " some good did come of it. When the chickens pecked the apple to pieces the seeds fell out, and one seed crept under a clover leaf where the chickens could not find it. And when the snow had lain all winter upon the earth, and the spring came, this little seed sprouted and grew, and sent down roots and sent up leaves, and became an apple-tree."

" How soon ? " said Carl.

" O in the course of years—by the time Mark was a big boy. And the tree blossomed and bore fruit; and from that time Mark and his mother never wanted for apples. He called it the 'Thanksgiving Tree,' but it was a true Beach-amwell, for all that."

"But say!" exclaimed Carl, catching hold of Beachamwell's stem in his great interest, "Mark isn't alive now, is he?"

"No," said Beachamwell, twisting away from Carl and her stem together. "No, he is not alive now, but the tree is, and it belongs to Mark's grandson. And the other day he picked a whole wagon-load of us and set off to market; and we three were so tired jolting about that we rolled out and lay by the wayside. That's where your mother found us."

"Well that is certainly a very pretty story," said Carl, "but nevertheless I'm glad my stocking was full. But I will let you Beachamwell and Half-ripe and Knerly lie on the chest and hear the rest of the stories, for I like this one very much."

Carl was tired sitting still by this time, so he went out and ran about on the beach till dinner; and after dinner he went up to his corner again. The sun came in through the little window, look-askance at Carl's treasures, and giving a strange, old-fashioned air to purse and book and stocking.

The shoes looked new yet, and shone in their blacking, and the apples had evidently but just quitted the tree; while the red cent gleamed away in the fair light, and the old pine cone was brown as ever, and reflected not one ray. Carl handled one thing and another, and then his eye fell on his small portion of money. He might want to spend it!—therefore if the cent could do anything, it must be done at once; and as he thought on the subject, the sun shone in brighter and brighter, and the red cent looked redder and redder. Then the sunbeam fled away, and only a dark little piece of copper lay on the chest by the side of the new shoes.

"Now red cent," said Carl, "it is your turn. I'll hear you before the purse, so make haste."

"Turn me over then," said the red cent, " for I can't talk with my back to people."

So Carl turned him over, and there he lay and stared at the ceiling.

THE STORY OF THE RED CENT.

" I cannot begin to relate my history," said
the red cent, " without expressing my astonishment at the small consideration in which I am
had. ' I wouldn't give a red cent for it—.' ' It isn't
worth a red cent—' such are the expressions
which we continually hear; and yet truly a man
might as well despise the particles of flour that
make up his loaf of bread.

" People say it is pride in me—that may be
and it may not. But if it be—why shouldn't a
red cent have at least that kind of pride which
we call self-respect? I was made to be a red
cent, I was wanted to be a red cent, I was never
expected to be anything else—therefore why
should I be mortified at being only a red cent?
I am all that I was intended to be, and a silver
dollar can be no more. Pride, indeed! why
even Beachamwell here is proud, I dare say, and

only because she is not a russeting; while I think—— Well, never mind,—but I have bought a good many apples in my day and ought to know something about them. *Only* a red cent! People can't bargain so well without me, I can tell you. Just go into the market to buy a cabbage, or into the street to buy a newspaper, and let me stay at home—see how you will fare then. Indeed when there is question of parting with me I am precious enough in some people's eyes, but it hardly makes up for the abuse I get from other quarters. There is indeed one pretty large class of the community who always think me worth picking up, though they are over ready to part with me. To them alone would I unfold the secrets of my past life. I might have lain in a man's purse for ever, and rubbed down all the finer parts of my nature against various hard-headed coins; but there is something in the solitude of a boy's pocket which touches all the sympathies of our nature—even beforehand.

"I am not, however," continued the red cent, "I am not at all of friend Beachamwell's temperament,—in fact I never had but one impression made on me in my life. To be sure that was permanent, and such as Time only can efface; though no doubt he will one day soften down my most prominent points, and enable me to move through society with a calm and even exterior. For it happens, oddly enough, that while beneath the pressure of years the 'human face divine' grows wrinkled and sometimes sharp, a red cent grows smooth and polished,— a little darker and thinner perhaps than formerly, but with as good business faculties as ever.

" When that time arrives," said the red cent, " we refuse to tell our age ; but until then we are perfectly communicative. I would at once tell you how old I am, but that you can see for yourself.

" I shall not give you a detailed account of my origin, nor of the fire and water through which I passed in order to become a red cent. If when you grow up you are still curious about the matter, you may cross over to England ; and there, down in Cornwall, you will find what may be called my birthplace, and can learn with full particulars why I left it. Neither shall I relate how I was pressed and clipped and weighed at the Mint, nor speak of the first few times that I went to market and changed hands. My present history will begin with the pocket of a rich old gentleman, into which I found my way one after noon along with a large variety of the ' circulating medium.' "

" You do use such big words ! " said Carl.

" Because I have travelled a great deal," said the red cent.   " It is the fashion.   But to return to the pocket.

" What a pocket it was !

" At the bottom lày an overfed pocket-book, bursting with bank-bills new and old, while another of like dimensions held more value, snugly stowed away in notes and bonds.   The leather purse in which I lay had one end for red cents and the other for gold and silver ; but with my usual love of bright company, when the old gentleman slipped me in among a parcel of dingy cents I slipped out again, and ran in among the half-eagles.   For I was the only new cent the old gentleman had, and as by right I belonged about half to him and half to the bank, the cashier and he had some words as to which should carry me off.   I believe the old gentleman chuckled over me half the way home.

" If this part of my story teaches nothing else," said the red cent with a moralising air as he stared at the ceiling, " it will at least show the folly of going out of one's proper place.   Had I been content to lodge with the red cents, I should but have been set to do a red cent's work,—as it was I was made to do the work of an eagle, for which I was totally unfit. It fell out thus.

" The old gentleman walked leisurely home, having very much the air of a man with a pocket full of money,—as I should think from the deliberate and comfortable way in which we were jogged about; and when he rang his own door bell it was already quite dark. A dear little girl opened the door, dressed in a white frock and black apron.

" ' Oh, grandpa,' she said, ' I'm so glad you've come, because there's a little boy been waiting here ever so long for ten dollars.'

" ' Well my dear,' said the old gentleman, ' ten dollars is worth waiting for.'

" ' But he's in a great hurry to get home before dark, because he says the children have got no bread for supper till he buys it,' said the little girl. ' He brought a pair of boots and shoes for you, grandpa. His father's very poor, he says.'

" ' Is he ? ' said the old gentleman. ' Then I'm afraid my boots won't be worth much. However Nanny my dear, you may take him the money for 'em, since they're here.'

" ' Shall I fetch you a light, grandpa ?' said the child. ' It's too dark to see.'

" ' No, no—not a bit of it,—I know how ten dollars feels, well enough. He shall have a gold piece—for the first time in his life, I'll warrant. It *is* too dark to read bank-bills.'

" And opening the most precious end of his purse, the old gentleman's unerring thumb and finger drew forth *me*, and laid me in the little girl's open palm. The soft little hand closed upon me, and down she ran to the lower entry.

" ' There—' she said,—' here it is. Grandpa says he guesses that's the first gold piece you ever had. Have you got a great many little brothers and sisters ?'

" ' This ain't gold,' said the boy, too busy examining me to heed her last question. ' He's made a mistake—this is only a red cent.'

" ' O well I'll take it back to him then,' said the little messenger. ' I s'pose he couldn't see in the dark.' And away she ran.

" The old gentleman by this time was enjoying his slippers and the newspaper, between a blazing fire and two long candles in tall silver candlesticks.

" ' Grandpa,' said the child laying her hand on his knee, ' do you know what you did in the dark? you gave that boy a red cent instead of a gold piece—wasn't it funny?'

"'Hey! what?' said the old gentleman, moving his paper far enough to one side to see the little speaker. 'Gave him a cent instead of a gold piece? nonsense!'

"'But you did, grandpa,' urged the child. 'See here—he gave it right back to me. It was so dark, you know, and he took it to the window to look; and he said directly it was only a cent.'

"'Which he had kept in his hand for the purpose, I'll warrant,' said the old man. 'Took it to the window, did he?—yes, to slip it into his pocket. He needn't think to play off that game upon me.'

"'But only look at it, grandpa,' said the child; 'see—it's only a red cent. I'm sure he didn't change it.'

"'I don't want to look at it,' said he putting away her hand. 'All stuff, my dear—it was as good an eagle as ever came out of the Mint. Don't I know the feel of one? and didn't I take it out of the gold end of my purse, where I *never* put copper? Bad boy, no doubt—you mustn't go back to him. Here, William—'

"'But he looked good, grandpa,' said the child, 'and so sorry.'

" ' He'll look sorry now, I'll be bound,' said the old man. 'I say, William!—take this red cent back to that boy, and tell him to be off with it, and not to show his face here again.'

" The command was strictly obeyed; and my new owner after a vain attempt to move the waiter, carried me into the street and sat down on the next door-step. Never in my life have I felt so grieved at being only a red cent, as then.

" The boy turned me over and over, and looked at me and read my date with a bewildered air, as if he did not know what he was doing; and I alas, who could have testified to his honesty, had no voice to speak.

" At length he seemed to comprehend his loss; for dropping me on the pavement he sank his head on his hands, and the hot tears fell fast down from his face upon mine. Then, in a sudden passion of grief and excitement he caught me up and threw me from him as far as he could; and I, who had been too proud to associate with red cents, now fell to the very bottom of an inglorious heap of mud. As I lay there half smothered, I could hear the steps of the boy, who soon repenting of his rashness now sought me—inasmuch as I was better than nothing; but he sought in vain. He couldn't see me and I couldn't see

him, especially as there was little but lamplight
to see by, and he presently walked away.

· "I am not good at reckoning time," said the
red cent, "but I should think I might have lain
there about a week—the mud heap having in the
mean time changed to one of dust; when a fu-
rious shower arose one afternoon, or I should
rather say came down; and not only were dust
and mud swept away, but the rain even washed
my face for me, and left me almost as bright as
ever high and dry upon a clean paving-stone.

"I felt so pleased and refreshed with being able
to look about once more, that what next would
become of me hardly cost a thought; and very
wet and shiny I lay there, basking in the late
sunshine."

"I thought you said you were high and dry?"
said Carl.

"That is a phrase which we use," replied the
red cent. "I was high and dry in one sense,—
quite lifted above the little streams of water that
gurgled about among the paving-stones, though
the rain-drops were not wiped off my face; and
as I lay there I suddenly felt myself picked up
by a most careful little finger and thumb, which
had no desire to get wet or muddy. They belonged to a little girl about ten years old.

" 'You pretty red cent!' she said, admiringly,—
'how bright and nice you do look! and how
funny it is that I should find you—I never found
anything before. I wonder how you came here
—I hope some poor child didn't lose you.'

" While she thus expressed her opinion I was
busy making up mine, and truly it was a pleasant
one. Her calico frock was of an indescribable
brown, formed by the fading together of all the
bright colours that had once enlivened it,—water
and soap and long wear had done this. But
water and soap had also kept it clean, and a very
little starch spread it out into some shape, and
displayed the peculiar brown to the best advan-
tage. Instead of an old straw bonnet with soiled
ribbons she had a neat little sun-bonnet; but
this was made of a piece of new pink calico, and
made her face look quite rosy. I could not see
her feet and pantalettes, for my back was towards
them, but I have no doubt they were in nice
order — she was too nice a child to have it other-
wise. Her hair was brushed quite smooth, only
when she stooped to pick me up one lock had
fallen down from under the sun-bonnet; and her
face was as simple and good as it could be. With
what contented eyes did she look at me! She
didn't wish I was an eagle — indeed I thought it

doubtful whether she had ever heard of such a thing. But I saw that her cheeks were thin, and that they might have been pale but for the pink sun-bonnet. Whatever *she* meant by 'a poor child,' little Nanny would surely have given the name to her.

"Suddenly she exclaimed,—

"'Now I can get it!—O I'm so glad! Come little red cent, I must give you away, though I should like to keep you very much, for you're very pretty; but you are all the money I've got in the world.'

"'Now for the candy-store,' thought I; for as she turned and began to walk away as fast as she could, I peeped into the little basket that hung on her arm and saw there a small loaf of bread—so I knew I was not to go for that commodity. She did not put me in the basket, but kept me fast in her hand as she tripped along, till we came to a large grocery. There she went in.

"'Please sir to let me have a cent's worth of tea?' she said timidly.

"'Got sixpence to pay for it?' said one of the clerks to make the other clerks laugh, in which he succeeded.

"'No sir, I've got this,' she said, modestly showing me, and giving me a kind glance at the

same time. ' It's only a cent, but it will get
enough for mother, and she's sick and wanted
some tea so much.'

" The young men stopped laughing, and looked
at the child as if she had just come out of the mu-
seum; and one of them taking down a canister
measured out two or three good pinches of tea into
a brown paper and folded it up. The child took it
with a very glad face, laying me down on the
counter with a joyful ' Thank you, sir!' which I
by no means repeated—I wanted to go home with
her and see that tea made. But we red cents can
never know the good that our purchases do in
the world.

" The clerk took me up and balanced me upon
his finger, as if he had half a mind to give the
child back her money, and pay the sum of one
cent into the store out of his own private purse.
But habit prevailed; and dropping me into the
till I heard him remark as he closed it,—

" ' I say, Bill, I shouldn't wonder now if that
was a good child.'

" I shouldn't have wondered, either.

" We were a dull company in the till that night,
for most of the money was old; and it is a well-
known fact that worn-down coins are not communicative. And some of the pieces were rusty

through long keeping, and one disconsolate little sixpence which sat alone in the furthest corner of the till, was in a very sad state of mind; for he had just laid himself out to buy some rice for a poor family and now could do nothing more for them—and he was the last monied friend they had.

" In this inactive kind of life some time passed away, and though some of us were occasionally taken to market yet we never bought anything. But one evening a man came into the grocery and asked for starch, and we hoped for bright visiters; but I had no time to enjoy them, for I was sent to make change. The messenger was a manservant, and with the starch in his hand and me in his pocket he soon left the store and went whistling along the street. Then he put his other hand into the pocket and jingled me against the rest of the change in a most unpleasant manner—picking me up and dropping me again just as if red cents had no feeling. I was glad when he reached home, and ran down the area steps and into the kitchen. He gave the starch to the cook, and then marking down on a little bit of paper what he had bought and what he had spent, he carried it with the change into the parlour. But what was my surprise to find that I was in

the very same house whence I had gone forth as
a golden eagle!

" The old gentleman was asleep in his chair now,
and a pretty-looking lady sat by, reading; while
the little girl was playing with her doll on the
rug. She jumped up and came to the table, and
began to count the change.

" ' Two-and-sixpence, mamma — see, here's a
shilling and two sixpences and a fivepence and
a red cent,—mamma, may I have this cent?'

" ' It isn't mine, Nanny—your grandfather gave
James the money.'

" ' Well, but you can pay him again,' said the
child ; ' and besides, he'd let me have it, I know.'

" ' What will you do with it, Nanny ?'

" ' Don't you know, mamma, you said you *thought*
you would give me one cent a month to spend ?'

" ' To do what you liked with,' said her mother.
' Yes, I remember. But what will you do with
this one ?'

" ' O I don't know, mamma—I'll see if grandpa will let me have it.'

" ' Let you have what ?' said the old gentleman,
waking up.

" ' This cent, grandpa.'

" ' To be sure you may have it ! Of course !—
and fifty more.'

" ' No, she must have but one,' said the lady, with a smile. ' I am going to give her an allowance of one cent a-month.'

" ' Fiddle-de-dee!' said the old gentleman. ' What can she do with that, I should like to know?—one red cent!—Absurd!'

" ' Why she can do just the fiftieth part of what she could with half-a-dollar,' said the lady, ' and that will be money matters enough for such a little head. So you may take the cent, Nanny, and spend it as you like,—only I shall want to be told about it afterwards.'

" Nanny thanked her mother, and holding me fast in one hand she sat down on the rug again by her doll. The old gentleman seemed very much amused.

" ' What will you do with it, Nanny?' he said, bending down to her.—' Buy candy?'

" Nanny smiled and shook her head.

" ' No, I guess not, grandpa—I don't know—I'll see. Maybe I'll buy beads.'

" At which the old gentleman leaned back in his chair and laughed very heartily.

" From that time, whenever little Nanny went to walk I went too; and she really seemed to be quite fond of me, for though she often stopped before the candy stores or the toy shops, and once or

E

twice went in to look at the beads, yet she always
carried me home again

" 'Mamma, I don't know how to spend my red
cent,' she said one day.

" 'Are you tired of taking care of it, Nanny ?'

" 'No mamma, but I want to spend it.'

" 'Why ?'

" 'Why mamma—I don't know — money's
meant to spend, isn't it ?'

" 'Yes, it is meant to spend—not to throw away.'

" 'O no,' said Nanny,—'I wouldn't throw
away my red cent for anything. It's a very pretty
red cent.'

" 'How many ways are there of throwing away
money ?' said her mother.

" 'O mamma—a great many ! I couldn't begin
to count. You know I might throw it out of the
window, mamma, or drop it in the street—or somebody might steal it,—no, then it would only be
lost.'

" 'Or you might shut it up in your box and
never spend it.'

" 'Why mamma !' said Nanny opening her eyes
very wide, ' would it be thrown away then ?'

" 'Certainly—you might just as well have none.
It would do neither you nor any one else any
good.'

" ' But I should have it to look at.'

" ' But that is not what money was made for. Your cent would be more really lost than if you threw it out of the window, for then some poor child might pick it up.'

" ' How surprised she would be!' said Nanny with a very bright face. ' Mamma, I think I should like to spend my money so. I could stand behind the window-curtain and watch.'

" Her mother smiled.

" ' Why, mamma? do you think there wouldn't any poor child come along?'

" ' I should like to see that day, dear Nanny. But your cent *might* fall into the grass in the courtyard, or into the mud, or a horse might tread it down among the paving-stones; and then no one would be the better for it.'

" ' But it's only one cent, mamma,' said Nanny, —' it don't matter so much, after all.'

" ' Come here Nanny,' said her mother, and the child came and stood at her side. The lady opened her purse and took out a little gold dollar.

" ' What is this made of?' said she

" ' Why of gold, mamma.'

" ' Think again.'

" So Nanny thought and couldn't think—and

laid her head against her mother, and played with the little gold dollar. Then she laid it upon me to see how much smaller it was, and how much brighter. Then she cried out,—

" 'O I know now, mamma! it's made of a hundred cents.'

" ' Then if every day you lose ' only a cent,' in one year you would have lost more than three dollars and a-half. That might do a great deal of good in the world.'

" ' How funny that is!' said Nanny. 'Well I 'll try and not lose my cent, mamma.'

" ' There is another reason for not losing it,' said her mother. 'In one sense it would make little difference whether or not I threw this little gold dollar into the fire—you see there are plenty more in my purse. But Nanny they do not belong to me.' And taking up a Bible she read these words,—

" ' *The silver and gold are* THE LORD'S.'

" ' Do you think, Nanny, that it pleases him to have us waste or spend foolishly what he has given us to do good with?'

" ' No mamma. I won't get my beads then,' said Nanny with a little sigh.

" ' That would not be waste,' said her mother kissing her. 'It is right to spend some of our

"' Mamma! did you see that little girl on those brown steps? ' "
P. 53.

money for harmless pleasure, and we will go and buy the beads this very afternoon.'

" So after dinner they set forth.

" It was a very cold day, but Nanny and her mother were well wrapped up, so they did not feel it much. Nanny's fur tippet kept all the cold wind out of her neck, and her little muff kept one hand warm while the other was given to her mamma. When that got cold Nanny changed about, and put it in the muff and the other out. As for me I was in the muff all the time ; and I was just wondering to myself what kind of a person the bead-woman would prove to be, when I heard Nanny say,—

" ' Mamma ! did you see that little girl on those brown steps ? She had no tippet, mamma, and not even a shawl, and her feet were all tucked up in her petticoat ; and——' and Nanny's voice faltered—' I think she was crying. I didn't look at her much, for it made me feel bad, but I thought so.'

" ' Yes love,' said her mother, ' I saw her. How good God has been to me, that it is not my little daughter who is sitting there.'

" ' O mamma !'

" Nanny walked on in silence for about half a block—then she spoke again.

" ' Mamma—I'm afraid a great many poor children want things more than I want my beads.'

" ' I'm afraid they do, Nanny.'

" ' Mamma, will you please go back with me and let me give that little girl my red cent? wouldn't she be pleased, mamma? would she know how to spend it?'

" ' Suppose you spend it for her, Nanny. People that are cold are often hungry too—shall we go to the baker's and buy her something to eat?'

" ' O yes!' said Nanny. 'Will you buy it, mamma, or shall I?'

" ' You, darling.'

" And when they reached the shop Nanny looked round once more at her mother, and opening the shop-door with a very pleased and excited little face she marched up to the counter.

" ' If you please, sir,' she said, laying me down on the counter, 'I want something for a very poor little girl.'

" The baker was a large fat man, in the whitest of shirt-sleeves and aprons, and the blackest pantaloons and vest, over which hung down a heavy gold watch-chain. He put his hands on his sides and looked at Nanny, and then at me, and then at Nanny again.

" ' *What* do you want, my dear?' said he.

" Nanny looked round at her mother to reassure herself, and repeated her request.

" ' I want something for a very poor little girl, if you please, sir. She's sitting out in the street all alone.' And Nanny's lips were trembling at the remembrance. Her mother's eyes were full too.

" ' What will you have, my dear?' said the baker.

" Nanny looked up at her mother.

" ' What would you like if you were hungry?' replied her mother.

" ' O I should like some bread,' said Nanny, ' and I guess the little girl would, too. But all those loaves are too big.'

" ' How would these do?' said the baker, taking some rolls out of a drawer.

" ' O they're just the thing!' said Nanny, ' and I like rolls so much. May I take one sir? and is a cent enough to pay for it?'

" The baker gave a queer little shake of his head, and searching below the counter for a bit of wrapping-paper he laid the two largest rolls upon it.

" ' A cent is enough to pay for two,' he said. ' Shall I tie them up for you?'

" ' No thank you sir; you needn't tie it—if

you'll only wrap them up a little. Mamma,' said Nanny, turning again to her mother, 'I'm afraid that poor little girl don't know that 'the silver and gold are the Lord's,' and she'll only think that I gave it to her.'

"'You can tell her, Nanny, that everything we have comes from God,' said her mother; and they left the shop."

"What a nice little girl!" said Carl. "I think I should like to marry that little girl when I grow up—if I was good enough."

"The baker went right into the back room," continued the red cent, "to tell the story to his wife, and I was left to my own reflections on the counter; but I had reason to be well satisfied, for it was certainly the largest cent's worth I had ever bought in my life. But while I lay there thinking about it, a boy came into the shop; and seeing me, he caught me up and ran out again. At least he was running out, when he tripped and fell; and, as I am noted for slipping through people's fingers, I slipped through his, and rolled to the furthest corner of the shop. There I lay all night; and in the morning when the baker's boy was sweeping the floor, he found me and put me in the till, for he was honest. But just then Mr. Krinken came in with a string of fish, and

the careless creature gave me with some other
change for a parcel of miserable flounders. That's
the way I came here."

"Why was he a careless boy?" said Carl. "I
think he was very careful, to find you at all."

"O because I didn't want to quit the baker,
I suppose," said the red cent. "And I don't like
the smell of fish, anyhow—it don't agree with
me."

"You won't smell much of it when I've kept
you awhile in my purse,' said Carl. "I'll take
good care of you, red cent, and I won't spend you
till I want to"

———

The next day Carl had tired himself with a run
on the sands. He used to tuck up his trowsers as
high as they would go, and wade slowly in through
the deepening water, to pick up stones and shells
and feel the little waves splash about his legs.
Then when a bigger wave than usual came rolling
in, black and high, to break further up on the
shore than the other great waves did, Carl would
run for it, shouting and tramping through the
water, to see if he could not get to land before the

breaker which came rolling and curling so fast
after him. Sometimes he did; and sometimes
the billow would curl over and break just a little
behind him, and a great sea of white foam would
rush on over his shoulders and maybe half hide
his own curly head. Then Carl laughed louder than
ever. He didn't mind the wetting with salt
water. And there was no danger, for the shore
was very gently shelving and the sand was white
and hard; and even if a big wave caught him up
off his feet and cradled him in towards the shore,
which sometimes happened, it would just leave
him there, and never think of taking him back
again; which the waves on some beaches would
certainly do.

All this used to be in the summer weather; at
Christmas it was rather too cold to play tag with
the breakers in any fashion. But Carl liked their
company, and amused himself in front of them,
this sunny December day, for a long time. He
got tired at last, and then sat himself flat down
on the sand, out of reach of the water, to rest
and think what he would do next. There he
sat, his trowsers still tucked up as far as they
would go, his little bare legs stretched out towards
the water, his curls crisped and wetted with a
dash or two of the salt wave, and his little ruddy

face, sober and thoughtful, pleasantly resting, and gravely thinking what should be the next play. Suddenly he jumped up, and the two little bare feet pattered over the sand and up on the bank, till he reached the hut.

"What ails the child!" exclaimed Mrs. Krinken.

But Carl did not stop to tell what. He made for the cupboard, and climbed up on a chair and lugged forth with some trouble, from behind everything, a clumsy wooden box. This box held his own treasures and nobody else's. A curious boxful it was. Carl soon picked out his Christmas purse; and without looking at another thing shut the box, pushed it back, swung to the cupboard door, and getting down from his chair ran back, purse in hand, the way he came, the little bare feet pattering over the sand, till he reached the place where he had been sitting; and then down he sat again just as he was before, stretched out his legs towards the sea, and put the purse down on the sand between them.

"Now purse," said he, "I 'll hear your story Come,—tell."

THE STORY OF THE PURSE.

" I don't feel like story-telling," said the purse.
" I have been opening and shutting my mouth all
my life, and I am tired of it."

The purse looked very snappish.

" Why you wouldn't be a purse if you couldn't
open and shut your mouth," said Carl.

" Very true," said the other ; " but one may be
tired of being a purse, mayn't one ?   I am."

" Why ? " said Carl.

" My life is a failure."

" I don't know what that means," said Carl.

" It means that I never have been able to do
what I was meant to do, and what I have all my
life been trying to do."

" What's that ? " said Carl.

" Keep money."

" You shall keep my cent for me," said Carl.

" Think of that !   A   red   cent !   Anything

might hold a red cent. I am of no use in the world."

" Yes, you are," said Carl,—" to carry my cent."

" You might carry it yourself," said the purse.

" No, I couldn't," said Carl. " My pockets are full."

" You might lose it, then. It's of no use to keep one cent. You might as well have none."

" No, I mightn't," said Carl; " and you've got to keep it: and you've got to tell me your story, too."

" Maybe you'll lose me," said the purse. " I wish your mother had."

" No, I sha'n't lose you," said Carl; and he lifted up his two legs on each side of the purse and slapped them down in the sand again;—" I sha'n't lose you."

" It wouldn't be the first time," said the purse.

" Were you ever lost ? " said Carl.

" Certainly I was."

" Then how did you get here ? "

" That's the end of my story — not the beginning."

" Well, make haste and begin," said Carl.

" The first place where I was settled was in a big fancy-store in London," the purse began.

"Where were you before that?" said Carl.

"I was in one or two rooms where such things are made, and where I was made."

"Where were you before that?"

"I wasn't a purse before that. I wasn't anywhere."

"What are you made of?" said Carl shortly.

"I am made of sealskin, the sides, and my studs and clasp are silver."

"Where did the sides and the clasp come from?"

"How should I know?" said the purse.

"I didn't know but you did," said Carl.

"I don't," said the purse.

"Well, go on," said Carl. "What did you do in that big shop?"

"I did nothing. I lay in a drawer, shut up with a parcel of other purses."

"Were they all sealskin, with silver clasps?"

"Some of them; and some were morocco and leather, with steel clasps."

"I'm glad you have got silver clasps," said Carl,—"you look very bright."

For Mrs. Krinken had polished up the silver of the clasp and of every stud along the seams, till they shone again.

"I feel very dull now," said the purse. "But

in those days I was as bright as a butterfly, and as handsome. My sides were a beautiful bright red."

" I don't believe it," said Carl; " they are not red a bit now."

" That's because I have been rubbed about in the world till all my first freshness is worn off. I am an old purse, and have seen a good deal of wear and tear."

" You aren't torn a bit," said Carl.

" If you don't shut up, I will," said the purse.

" I won't," said Carl. " And you've got to go on."

" The next place I was in was a gentleman's pocket."

" How did you get there?"

" He came to buy a purse, and so a number of us were thrown out upon the counter, and he looked at us and tried us, and bought me and put me in his pocket."

" What did you do there?"

" There my business was to hold guineas and half-guineas, and crowns and half-crowns, and all sorts of beautiful pieces of silver and gold."

" And cents?" said Carl.

" Not such a thing. My master hadn't any. He threw all his pennies away as fast as he got 'em."

"Threw 'em where?" said Carl.

"Anywhere — to little boys, and beggars, and poor people, and gate-openers, and such like."

"Why didn't he keep 'em?"

"He had enough besides — gold and silver. He didn't want pennies and halfpennies."

"I wish you had kept some of them," said Carl.

"I never had them to keep. I couldn't keep but what he gave me, nor that either. He was always taking out and putting in."

"Did *he* wear the red off?" said Carl.

"No. I didn't stay long enough with him. He was travelling in some part of England with a friend, riding over a wide lonely plain one day; and they saw a little distance ahead a cow in the road, lying down, right across their path. 'Stapleton,' said my master, 'let us clear that cow.' 'Can't your servant do that?' said Mr. Stapleton. 'Do what?' said my master. 'Clear that beast from the road,' said his friend. 'Pshaw!' said my master, — 'I mean, let us clear her at a bound. Leave her in quiet possession of the road, and we take an air-line over her back.' 'Suppose she took a stupid notion to get out of our way just as we are in hers?' said Mr. Stapleton. 'I don't suppose anything of the kind,' said my master; 'we shall be too quick for her.'

With that they put spurs to their horses, but it happened that Mr. Stapleton's horse got the start and was a little ahead. *He* cleared the cow well enough, but, unluckily it gave her an impression that just where she was it was a poor place to be ; and she was throwing up her hind legs at the very minute my master came to take the leap. He was flung over and over, he and his horse, over and under each other—I don't know how. I only know my master was killed.

"His friend and his servant picked him up and laid him by the roadside ; and while Mr. Stapleton went full speed to the nearest town to get help, the other stayed behind to take care of his master, and do what could be done for him. But he very soon found that nothing could be done for him ; and then, as nobody was in sight, he took the opportunity to do what he could for himself, by rifling his master's pockets. He pulled out several things which I suppose he didn't dare to keep, for he put them back again after a careful look at them, and after carefully taking off some seals from the watch-chain. I did not fare so well. He had me in his hands a long time, taking out and putting in silver and gold pieces, — afraid to keep too much, and not willing to leave a crown that might be kept

F

safely; when a sudden step heard near, and the bursting out of a loud whistle, startled him. He jumped as if he had been shot; which was natural enough, as he was running a pretty good chance of getting hanged. I was dropped, or thrown behind him, in the grass; and before the countryman who came up had done asking questions, the horses of Mr. Stapleton and assistants were seen over the rising ground. They carried away my unfortunate first master, and left me in the grass.

" I knew I shouldn't stay there long, but I was found sooner than I hoped. Before the evening had closed in, the sun was shining yet, I heard the tread of light feet, — somebody nearing the road and then crossing it. In crossing, this somebody came just upon me; and a kind sunbeam touching one of my silver points, I embraced the opportunity to shine as hard as I could. People say it is dangerous to have bright parts; I am sure I never found it out. I shone so she could not help seeing me. It was a girl about fifteen or sixteen years old: a slim figure, very tidy in her dress, with light brown hair nicely put back from her face; and her face a very quiet, sweet one. She looked at me, inside and out, looked up and down the road, as if to see where I had come from, and finally put me in her pocket. I was very glad nobody was in sight anywhere, for I knew by her face she would have given me up directly. She left the road then, and went on over the common, which was a wide, lonely, barren plain, grass-grown, and with here and there a bunch of bushes, or a low stunted tree. She was going after her cows, to bring them home; and presently, seeing them in the distance, she stood still and began to call them."

" How did she call them ?" said Carl.

" 'Cuff, cuff, cuff!' That was while they were a good way off; when they came near,—'Sukey' and ' Bessie,' and ' Jenny.'"

" And did they come when she called?"

" Left off eating as soon as they heard her; and then, when they had looked a little while to make sure it was she, they walked off slowly to come up to her."

" How many cows were there ?" said Carl.

" Sukey was a great black cow, and always marched first. Dolly was a beautiful red cow, and always was second. Three more came after her in a line, and when they got up with their little mistress she set off to go home, and the whole five of them followed gravely in order.

" The common was smooth and wide, not much broken with ups and downs and little footpaths—

or cow-paths—tracking it in all directions. We
wound along, my mistress and the cows, and I in
my mistress's pocket, through one and another of
these; passing nothing in the shape of a house
but a huge gloomy-looking building at some distance, which I afterwards found was a factory. A
little way beyond this, not more than a quarter of
a mile, we came to a small brown house, with one
or two out-buildings. The house stood in a little
field, and the out-buildings in another little field,
close beside this one. Everything was small ;
house, and barn, and shed, and cow-field, and
garden-field ; but it was all snug, and neat, too.

"My little mistress—for she was slender.
fair, and good, and such people we always call
little——"

"But she wasn't large, was she ?" said Carl.

"She was not as large as if she had been grown
up, but no more was she little for fifteen or sixteen. She was just right. She opened a gate of
the barnyard, and held it while all the five cows
marched slowly in, looking around them as if they
expected to see some change made in the arrange-
ments since they had gone out in the morning.
But the old shed and manger stood just where
they had left them, and Sukey stopped quietly in
the middle of the barnyard and began to chew

the cud, and Dolly and Bessie and Beauty took their stand in different places after her example; while Whiteface went off to see if she could find something in the mangers. She was an old cow that never had enough."

" Was Beauty a handsome cow?" said Carl.

" No, she was the ugliest one of the whole set; one of her horns was broken, and the other lopped down directly over her left eye."

" What was she called Beauty for, then?"

" Why, I heard say that she was a very pretty calf, and was named then in her youth; but when she grew older she took to fighting, and broke one of her horns, and the other horn bent itself down just in the wrong place. There is no knowing, while they are little, how calves or children will turn out.

" When their mistress had shut the gate upon the five cows, she opened another small gate in the fence of the field where the house stood; and there she went in, through two beds of roses and sweet herbs that were on each side of the narrow walk, up to the door. That stood open to let her in.

" It was the nicest place you ever saw. A clean scrubbed floor, with a thick coarse piece of carpet covering the middle of it; a dark wooden table and wooden chairs, nice and in their places, only one chair stood on the hearth, as if somebody had just left it. There was a big, wide, comfortable fire-place, with a fire burning in it, and over the fire hung a big iron tea-kettle, in the very midst of the flames, and singing already. On each side of the chimney brown wooden cupboards filled up the whole space from the floor to the ceiling. All tidy and clean. The hearth looked as if you might have baked cakes on it.

" The girl stood a minute before the fire, and then went to the inner door and called, ' Mother !'

" A pleasant voice from somewhere said, ' Here !'

" ' In the milk-room ?'

" ' Yes !'

" And my little mistress went along a short passage—brown it was, walls, and floor, and all, even the beams overhead—to the milk-room ; and that was brown, too, and as sweet as a rose.

" ' Mother, why did you put on the tea-kettle ?'

" ' 'Cause I wanted to have some tea, dear.'

" ' But I would have done it.'

" ' Yes, honey, I know. You've quite enough to do.'

" ' Look here what I've found, mother.'

" ' Can't look at anything, daughter. Go along and milk and I will hear you at tea-time.'

" Then my little mistress took up the pails, and
went out by another way, through another gate that
opened directly into the cows' yard; and there
she stripped the yellow sweet milk into the pails,
from every one of the five cows she had driven
home. Not one of them but loved to be milked
by her hand; they enjoyed it, every cow of
them; standing quiet and sleepily munching the
cud, except when now and then one of them
would throw back her head furiously at some fly
on her side; and then my mistress's soft voice
would say,—

" ' So, Beauty! '

" And Beauty was as good as possible to her,
though I have heard that other people did not
find her so.

" Mrs. Meadow took the milk-pails at the dairy
door, and my mistress came back into the kitchen
to get tea. She put up a leaf of the brown table
and set a tray on it, and out of one of the cupboards she fetched two tea-cups and saucers;
so I knew there were no more in the family.
Then two little blue-edged plates and horn-
handled knives, and the rest of the things; and
when the tea was made she dressed up the fire,
and stood looking at it and the tea-table by
turns, till her mother showed herself at the door,

and came in taking off her apron. She was the nicest-looking woman you ever saw."

" She wasn't as nice as my mother," said Carl.

" Mrs. Krinken never was half so nice. She was the best-natured, cheerfullest, pleasantest-faced woman you could find, as bright as one of her own red apples."

" Mine are bright," said Carl.

" Yours are bright for Christmas, but hers were bright for every day. Everything about her was bright. Her spoons, and the apples, and the brass candlesticks, and the milk-pans, and the glass in the windows, and·her own kind heart. The mother and daughter had a very cozy tea ; and I was laid upon the table and my story told, or rather the story of my being found ; and it was decided that I should remain in the keeping of the finder, whom her mother, by some freak of habit, rarely called anything but ' Silky.' "

" What for ?" said Carl.

" Maybe you'll find out if you don't ask so many questions," said the purse snappishly. 'It's yours, Silky,' Mrs. Meadow said, after looking at me and rubbing the silver mountings. ' It's odd such a handsome purse should have no money in it.'

" ' I'm not going to put it away out of sight.

mother,' said Silky; 'I'm going to have the good of it. I'll keep it to hold my milk-money.'

" ' Well, dear, here goes the first,' said Mrs. Meadow;—' here's a silver penny I took for milk while you were after the cows.'

" ' Who came for it, mother?'

" ' Don't know—a lady riding by—and she gave me this.'

" So a little silver coin was slipped into my emptiness, and my little mistress laid me on a shelf of the other cupboard, alongside of an old Bible. But she left the door a crack open; I could see them at work, washing up the tea-things, and then knitting and sewing upon the hearth, both of them by a little round table. By and by Mrs. Meadow took the Bible out and read, and then she and Silky kneeled down, close together, to pray. They covered up the fire after that, and shut the cupboard door, and went off to bed; and I was left to think what a new place I had come to, and how I liked it.

" It was a pretty great change. In my old master's pocket I had kept company with wealth and elegance—the tick of his superb watch was always in my ear; now, on Mrs. Meadow's cup-board shelf, I had round me a few old books, beside the Bible; an hour-glass; Mrs. Meadow's tin knitting-needle case; a very illiterate inkstand, and stumpy clownish old pen; and some other things that I forget. There I lay, day and night; from there I watched my two mistresses at their work and their meals; from thence I saw them, every night and morning, kneel together and pray; and there I learned a great respect for my neighbour the Bible. I always can tell now what sort of people I have got among, by the respect they have for it."

" My mother has one," said Carl.

" Her great chest knows that," said the purse. " I've been a tolerably near neighbour of that Bible for ten years; and it rarely gets leave to come out but on Sundays."

' She reads it on Sunday," said Carl.

' Yes, and puts it back before Monday. Mrs. Krinken *means* to be good woman, but these other people *were* good; there's all the difference.

" My business was to lie there on the shelf and keep the milk-pennies, and see all that was going on. Silky sold the milk. The people that came for it were mostly poor people from the neighbouring village, or their children going home from the factory; people that lived in poor little dwellings

in the town, without gardens or fields, or a cow
to themselves, and just bought a penny's worth,
or a halfpenny's, at a time—as little as they could
do with. There were a good many of these families, and among them they took a pretty good
share of the milk; the rest Mrs. Meadow made
up into sweet butter—*honest* sweet butter, she
called it, with her bright face and dancing eye;
and everything was honest that came out of her
dairy.

"The children always stopped for milk at night,
when they were going home; the grown people,
for the most part, came in the morning. After I
had been on the cupboard shelf awhile however,
and got to know the faces, I saw there was one
little boy who came morning and evening too.
In the morning he fetched a halfpennyworth and
in the evening a pennyworth of milk, in a stout
little brown jug; always the same brown jug; and
always in the morning he wanted a halfpennyworth and in the evening a pennyworth. He
was a small fellow, with a shock of red hair, and
his face all marked with the small-pox. He was
one of the poorest-looking that came. There was
never a hat on his head; his trowsers were fringed
with tags; his feet bare of shoes or stockings.
His jacket was always fastened close up; either

to keep him warm or to hide how very little there was under it. Poor little Norman Finch! That was his name.

"He had come a good many mornings. One day early, just as Mrs. Meadow and Silky were getting breakfast, his little red head poked itself in again at the door with his little brown jug, and 'Please, ma'am,—a ha'penn'orth.'

" 'Why don't you get all you want at once, Norman?' said Silky, when she brought the milk.

" 'I don't want only a ha'penn'orth,' said Norman.

" 'But you'll want a pennyworth to-night again, won't you?'

" 'I'll stop for it,' said Norman, casting his eyes down into the brown jug, and looking more dull than usual.

" 'Why don't you take it all at once, then?'

" 'I don't want it.'

" 'Have you got to go back home with this before you go work?'

" 'No——I must go,' said Norman, taking hold of the door.

" 'Are you going to the factory?'

" 'Yes, I be.'

" 'How will your mother get her milk?'

" 'She'll get it when I go home.'

" 'But not this, Norman. What do you want this for?'

" 'I want it—She don't want it,' said the boy, looking troubled,—' I must go.'

" 'Do you take it to drink at the factory?'

" 'No—It's to drink at the factory—She don't want it,' said Norman.

" He went off. But as Silky set the breakfast on the table she said,—

" 'Mother, I don't understand; I am afraid there is something wrong about this morning milk.'

" 'There's nothing wrong about it, honey,' said Mrs. Meadow, who had been out of the room; 'it's as sweet as a clover-head. What's the matter?'

" 'O, not the milk, mother; but Norman Finch's coming after it in the morning. He won't tell me what it's for; and they never used to take but a pennyworth a day, and his jug's always empty now at night; and he said it wasn't and it *was* to drink at the factory; and that his mother didn't want it; and I don't know what to think.'

" 'Don't think anything, dear,' said Mrs. Meadow, ' till we know something more. We'll

get the child to let it out.   Poor little creature!
I wish I could keep him out of that place.'

" ' Which place, mother?'

" ' I meant the factory "

" ' I don't believe he can have a good home,
mother, in his father's house. I am sure he can't.
That Finch is a bad man.'

" ' It's the more pity if it isn't a good home,'
said Mrs. Meadow, ' for it is very little he sees of
it.   It's too much for such a morsel of a creature
to work all day long.'

" ' But they are kind at the pin-factory, mother.
People say they are.'

" ' Mr. Carroll is a nice man,' said her mother.
' But nine hours is nine hours.   Poor little creature!'

" ' He looks thinner and paler now than he did
six months ago.'

" ' Yes; and then it was winter, and now it is
summer,' said Mrs. Meadow.

" ' I wish I knew what he wants to do with
that milk!' said Silky

" The next morning Norman was there again.
He put himself and his jug only half in at the
door, and said, somewhat doubtfully,—

" ' Please, ma'am, a ha'penn'orth ?'

" ' Come in, Norman,' said Silky.

" He hesitated.

" ' Come !—come in—come in to the fire; it's chilly out of doors. You're in good time, aren't you ?'

" ' Yes,—but I can't stay,' said the boy, coming in however, and coming slowly up to the fire. But he came close, and his two hands spread themselves to the blaze as if they liked it, and the poor little bare feet shone in the firelight on the hearth. It was early, very cool and damp abroad.

" ' I'll get you the milk,' said Silky, taking the jug;—'you stand and warm yourself. You've plenty of time.'

" She came back with the jug in one hand and a piece of cold bacon in the other, which she offered to Norman. He looked at it, and then grabbed it, and began to eat immediately. Silky stood opposite to him with the jug.

" ' What's this milk for, Norman?' she said, pleasantly.

" He stopped eating and looked troubled directly.

" ' What are you going to do with it ?'

" ' Carry it—home,' he said, slowly.

" ' Now?—home now? Are you going back with it now ?'

" ' I am going to take it to the factory.'

" ' What do you do with it there ? "

" ' Nothing,' said Norman, looking at his piece
of bacon, and seeming almost ready to cry ;—' I
don't do nothing with it?"

" 'You needn't be afraid to tell me, dear,' Silky
said, gently. ' I'm not going to do you any harm.
Does your mother know you get it ? '

" He waited a good while, and then when she
repeated the question, taking another look at
Silky's kind quiet face, he said half under his
breath,—

" ' No—'

" ' What do you want it for, then, dear ?   I'd
rather give it to you than have you take it in a
wrong way.—Do you want it to drink ? '

" Norman dropped his piece of bacon.

" ' No,' he said, beginning to cry,—' I don't
want it—I don't want it at all ! '—

" Silky picked up the bacon, and she looked
troubled in her turn.

" ' Don't cry, Norman,—don't be afraid of me.
—Who does want it?'

" ' Oh, don't tell !—' sobbed the child ;—' My
little dog !—'

" 'Now don't cry !' said Silky.—' Your little
dog ? '

" ' Yes!—my little dog.'— And he sighed deeply between the words.

" ' Where is your little dog?'

" ' He's up yonder—up to the factory.'

" ' Who gave him to you?'

" ' Nobody didn't give him to me. I found him.'

" ' And this milk is for him?'

" ' He wants it to drink.'

" ' Does your mother know you get it?'

" Norman didn't answer.

" ' She don't?' said Silky. ' Then where does the money come from, Norman?' She spoke very gently.

" ' It's mine,' said Norman.

" ' Yes, but where do you get it?'

" ' Mr. Swift gives it to me.'

" ' Is it out of your wages?'

" Norman hesitated, and then said ' Yes,' and began to cry again.

" ' What's the matter?' said Silky. ' Sit down and eat your bacon. I'm not going to get you into trouble.'

" He looked at her again and took the bacon, but said he wanted to go.

" ' What for?—it isn't time yet.'

" ' Yes—I want to see my little dog.'

" ' And feed him? Stop and tell me about him. What colour is he?'

" ' He's white all over.'

" ' What's his name?'

" ' Little Curly Long-Ears.'

" ' What do you call him ?—all that ?'

" ' I call him Long-Ears.'

" ' But why don't you feed him at home, Norman?'

" ' He lives up there.'

" ' And don't he go home with you?'

" ' No.'

" ' Why not?'

" ' Father wouldn't let him. He'd take him away, or do something to him.'

" Norman looked dismal.

" ' But where does he live?'

" ' He lives up to the factory.'

" ' But you can't have him *in* the factory.'

" ' Yes, I have him,' said Norman, ' because Mr. Carroll said he was to come in, because he was so handsome.'

" ' But he'll get killed in the machinery, Norman, and then you would be very sorry.'

" ' No, he won't get killed; he takes care: he knows he mustn't go near the 'chinery, and he doesn't; he just comes and lies down where I be.'

" ' And does Mr. Swift let him ? '

" ' He has to, 'cause Mr. Carroll said he was to.'

" ' But your money—where does it come from, Norman ? '

" ' Mr. Swift,' said Norman, very dismally.

" ' Then doesn't your mother miss it, when you carry home your wages to her ? '

" ' No.'

" ' She *must*, my child.'

" ' She don't, 'cause I carry her just the same I did before.'

" ' How can you, and keep out a ha'penny a-day ? '

" ' 'Cause I get more now—I used to have four-pence ha'penny, and now they give me fi'pence.'

" And Norman burst into a terrible fit of crying, as if his secret was out, and it was all up with him and his dog too.

" ' Give me the milk and let me go ! ' he exclaimed through his tears. ' Poor Curly !—poor Curly ! '

" ' Here 'tis,' said Silky, very kindly. ' Don't cry—I'm not going to hurt you or Curly either. Won't he eat anything but milk ?—won't he eat meat ? '

" ' No—he can't—'

" ' Why can't he ? '

" ' He don't like it.'

" ' Well; you run off to the factory now and give Curly his milk; and stop again to-morrow.'

" ' And won't you tell?' said Norman, looking up.

" ' I shall not tell anybody that will get you into trouble.   Run, now!'

" He dried his tears, and ran, fast enough, holding the little brown jug carefully at half-arm's length, and his bare feet pattering over the ground as fast as his short legs could make them.

" Silky stood looking gravely after him.

" ' I'm so sorry for him, mother!' she said. ' This won't do; it's very wrong, and he'll get himself into dreadful trouble besides.'

" ' Poor fellow!—we'll see, honey;—we'll try what we can do,' said Mrs. Meadow.

" The next morning Norman came again, and Mrs. Meadow was there.

" ' How is Long-Ears, Norman? and how are you?' she said cheerfully. But she did everything cheerfully.

" ' He's well,' said Norman, looking a little doubtfully at these civilities.

" ' And you are not well?' said Mrs. Meadow, kindly. ' Suppose you come and see me to-morrow?—it's Sunday, you know, and you have no work—will you? Come bright and early, and we'll have a nice breakfast, and you shall go to church with me, if you like.'

" Norman shook his head. ' Curly 'll want to see me,' he said.

" ' Well, about that just as you like. Come here to breakfast—*that* you can do. Mother 'll let you.'

" ' Yes, she'll let me,' said Norman, ' and I can go to see Long-Ears afterwards. You won't tell?' he added, with a glance of some fear

" ' Tell what?'

" ' About *him*,' said Norman, nodding his head in the direction of the factory.

" ' Long-Ears?—Not I! not a word.'

" So he set off, with a gleam of pleasure lighting up his little face, and making his feet patter more quick over the ground.

" ' Poor little creature!' Mrs. Meadow said again, most heartily, and this time the tear was standing in her eye.

" The next morning it rained,—steadily, constantly, straight up and down. But at the usual time Mrs. Meadow and Silky were getting breakfast.

" ' It does come down!' said Mrs. Meadow.

" ' I'm so sorry, mother,' said Silky; 'he won't come.'

" She had hardly turned her back to see to something at the fire, when there he was behind her, standing in the middle of the floor; in no Sunday dress, but in his everyday rags, and those wet through and dripping. How glad and how sorry both mother and daughter looked! They brought him to the fire and wiped his feet, and wrung the water from his clothes as well as they could: but they didn't know what to do; for the fire would not have dried him in all the day; and sit down to breakfast dry, with him soaking wet at her side, Mrs. Meadow could not. What to put on him was the trouble; she had no children's clothes at all in the house. But she managed. She stripped off his rags, and tacked two or three towels about him; and then over them wound a large old shawl, in some mysterious way, fastening it over the shoulders: in such a manner that it fell round him like a loose straight frock, leaving his arms quite free. Then, when his jacket and trowsers had been put to dry, they sat down to breakfast.

" In his odd shawl wrapper, dry and warm, little Norman enjoyed himself, and liked very much his cup of weak coffee, and bread and butter,

and the nice egg which Mrs. Meadow boiled for
him. But he did not eat like a child whose
appetite knew what to do with good things; he
was soon done; though after it his face looked
brighter and cheerier than it ever had done be
fore in that house.

" Mrs. Meadow left Silky to take care of the
breakfast things; and, drawing her chair up on
the hearth, she took the little boy on her lap and
wound her arms about him.

" ' Little Norman,' said she kindly, ' you won't
see Long Ears to-day.'

" ' No,' said Norman, with a sigh, in spite of
breakfast and fire,—' he will have to go without
me.'

" ' Isn't it good that there is one day in the
week when the poor little tired pin-boy can
rest ? '

" ' Yes—it is good,' said Norman, quietly; but
as if he was too accustomed to being tired to
take the good of it.

" ' This is God's day. Do you know who God
is, Norman ? '

" ' He made me,' said Norman,—' and every
body.'

" ' Yes, and every thing. He is the great
King over all the earth; and he is good, and he

has given us this day to rest and to learn to be good and please him. Can you read the Bible, Norman?'

" ' No, I can't read,' said Norman. ' Mother can.'

" ' You know the Bible is God's book, written to tell us how to be good; and whatever the Bible says we must mind, or God will be angry with us. Now the Bible says, ' *Thou shalt not steal.*' Do you know what that means?'

" Mrs. Meadow spoke very softly.

" ' Yes,' said Norman, swinging one little foot back and forward in the warm shine of the fire, —' I've heard it.'

" ' What does it mean?'

" ' I know,' said Norman.

" ' It is to take what does not belong to us. Now, since God has said that, is it quite right for you to take that money of your mother's to buy milk for Long-Ears?'

" ' It *isn't* her money!' said Norman, his face changing; ' and Long-Ears can't starve!'

" ' It is her money, Norman;—all the money you earn belongs to her, or to your father, which is the same thing. You know it does.'

" ' But Curly must have something to eat,' said Norman, bursting into tears. ' Oh, don't tell! oh, don't tell!—'

" ' Hush, dear,' said Mrs. Meadow's kind voice, and her kind hand on his head ;—' I'm not going to tell; but I want you to be a good boy and do what will please God, that you may be one of the lambs of the Good Shepherd's flock.—Do you know what I am talking about?'

" ' Yes—no—I don't know about the lambs,' said Norman.

" ' Do you know who Jesus Christ is?'

" ' No.'

" ' Poor little thing!' said Silky, and the tears fell from her face as she went from the fire to the table. Norman looked at her, and so did her mother, and then they looked at each other.

" ' Jesus Christ is your best friend, little Norman.'

" ' Is he?' said Norman, looking.

" ' Do you know what he has done for you, little pin-boy?'

" Norman looked, and no wonder, for Mrs. Meadow's eyes were running over full, and he did not know what to make of the dropping tears; but he shook his head.

" ' It's all told about in God's book, dear. Little Norman Finch, like everybody else, hasn't loved God, nor minded his commandments as he ought to do; and God would have punished us all, if Jesus Christ hadn't come down from heaven on purpose to take our punishment on himself, so that we might be saved.'

" ' How would he have punished us?' said Norman.

" ' He would have sent us away from him, for ever, to be in a miserable place, with devils and bad people, where we should see nothing good nor happy, and we shouldn't be good nor happy ourselves; it's a place so dreadful, it is called in the Bible *the lake that burns with fire;* and he would never let us come into his heaven, where God is, and Jesus Christ is, and the good angels, and all God's people are, and are all as good and happy as they can be.'

" ' And would I have been punished so?' said Norman.

" ' Yes,—the Bible says so; and every one will now, who won't believe and love Jesus Christ.'

" ' And did he go there?'

" ' Where?'

" ' To that place—that bad place—did he go there?'

" ' What, the Lord Jesus?'

" Norman nodded.

" ' Not there,—he is God; and he is called

the Son of God; he could not do that; but he
did this. He came to this world and was born
into this world a little child; and when he grew
up to be a man, he died a cruel death for you
and me—for you and me, little Norman.'

" ' And then will God not punish me now?'
said Norman.

" ' No, not a bit, if you will love the Lord
Jesus and be his child.'

" ' What did he do that for?' said Norman.

" ' Because he is so good he loved us, and
wanted to save us and bring us back to be his
children, and to be good and happy.'

" ' Does he love me?' said Norman.

" ' Yes, indeed,' said Mrs. Meadow. ' Do you
think he came to die for you and doesn't love
you? If you will love and obey him, he will love
you for ever, and take care of you;—better care
than any one else can.'

" ' There isn't anybody else to take care of
me,' said Norman. ' Mother can't, and father
don't, much. I wish I knew about that.'

" With a look, of wonder and interest, at her
daughter, Mrs. Meadow reached after her Bible,
without letting Norman down from her lap; and
turning from place to place, read to him the
story of Christ's death, and various parts of his

life and teaching. He listened, gravely and con stantly and intently, and seemed not to weary of it at all, till she was tired and obliged to stop. He made no remark then, but sat a little while with a sober face; till his own fatigue of days past came over him, and his eyelids drooped, and slipping from Mrs. Meadow's lap, he laid himself down on the hearth to sleep. They put something under his head and sat watching him, the eyes of both every now and then running over.

" ' How much do you think he understood, mother?' said Silky.

" ' I don't know,' said Mrs. Meadow, shaking her head.

" ' He listened, mother,' said Silky.

" ' Yes. I won't say anything more to him to-day. He's had enough.'

" And when the little sleeper awoke, they bent all their attention to giving him a pleasant day. He had a good dinner and a nice supper. His clothes were thoroughly dried; and Mrs. Meadow said when she put them on, that if she could only get a chance of a week-day, she would patch them up comfortably for him. Towards nightfall the rain stopped, and he went home dry and warm, and with a good piece of cheese and a loaf of plain gingerbread under his arm. When he was all ready to set out he paused at the door, and looking up at Mrs. Meadow said,—

" ' Does he say we mustn't do that?'

" ' Who, dear?'

" ' Does Jesus Christ say we mustn't do that?

" ' Do what?'

" ' Steal,' said Norman, softly.

" ' Yes, to be sure. The Bible says it, and the Bible is God's word; and Jesus said it over again when he was on the earth.'

" Norman stood a quarter of a minute, and then went out and closed the door.

" The next morning they looked eagerly for him. But he did not come. He stopped at evening, as usual, but Silky was just then busy and did not speak to him beyond a word. Tuesday morning he did not come. At night he was there again with his jug.

" ' How do you do, Norman?' said Mrs. Meadow, when she filled it, ' and how is Long-Ears?'

" But Norman did not answer, and turned to go.

" ' Come here in the morning, Norman,' Mrs. Meadow called after him.

" Whether he heard her or not, he did not shew

himself on his way to the factory next morning.
That was Wednesday.

" ' Norman hasn't been here these three days,
mother,' said Silky. ' Can it be he has made
up his mind to do without his halfpennyworth
of milk for the dog?'

" ' Little fellow!' said Mrs. Meadow, ' I
meant to have given it to him; skim milk would
do, I dare say; but I forgot to tell him Sunday; and I told him last night to stop, but he
hasn't done it. We'll go up there, Silky, and
see how he is, after dinner.'

" ' To the factory, mother?'

" ' Ay.'

" ' And I'll carry a little pail of milk along,
mother.'

" ' Well, honey, do.'

" After dinner they went, and I went in Silky's
pocket. The factory was not a great distance
from Mrs. Meadow's house, which stood half way
between that and the town. Mrs. Meadow asked
for Mr. Swift, and presently he came. Mrs.
Meadow was a general favourite, I had found
before; everybody spoke her fair; certainly she
did the same by everybody.

" ' Is little Norman Finch at work to-day,
Mr. Swift?'

" ' Norman Finch? Well, yes, ma'am, he's
to work,' said the overseer;—' he don't *do* much
work this day or so.'

" ' He's not just right well, Mr. Swift.'

" ' Well, no, I s'pose he isn't. He hasn't hard
work neither; but he's a poor little billet of a
boy.

" ' Is he a good boy, sir?'

" ' Average,' said Mr. Swift;—' as good as the
average. What, you're going to adopt him?'

" ' No, sir,' said Mrs. Meadow; ' I wanted to
ask a few questions about him.'

" ' I don't know any harm of him,' said Mr.
Swift. ' He's about like the common. Not
particularly strong in the head, nor anywhere
else, for that matter; but he is a good-feeling
child. Yes—now I remember. It's as much as
a year ago, that I was mad with him one day,
and was going to give the careless little rascal
a strapping for something,—I forget what; we
must keep them in order, Mrs. Meadow, let them
be what they will;—I was going to give it to him,
for something,—and a bold brave fellow in the
same room, about twice as big and six times as
strong as Norman, offered to take it and spare
him. *I* didn't care; it answered my purpose of
keeping order just as well that Bill Bollings

should have it as Norman Finch, if he had a mind;—and ever since that time Finch has been ready to lay down his body and soul for Bollings, if it could do him any service. He's a good-hearted boy, I do suppose.'

" Mrs. Meadow and Silky looked at each other.

" ' That's it, mother!' said Silky. ' That's why he understood and took it so quick.'

" ' What a noble boy, the other one!' said Mrs. Meadow.

" ' Ha? well—*that* was noble enough,' said Mr. Swift; ' but he's a kind of harum-scarum fellow—just as likely to get himself into a scrape to-morrow as to get somebody else out of one to-day.'

" ' That was noble,' repeated Mrs. Meadow.

" ' Norman has never forgotten it. As I said, he'd lay down body and soul for him. There's a little pet-dog he has, too,' Mr. Swift went on, ' that I believe he'd do as much for. A pretty creature! I would have bought it of him, and given a good price for it, but he seemed frightened at the proposal. I believe he keeps the creature here partly'for fear he would lose him home.'

" ' Isn't it against the rules, sir, to have a dog in the factory?'

" ' Entirely !—of course !' said Mr. Swift; 'but Mr. Carroll has said it, and so a new rule is made for the occasion. Mr. Carroll was willing to let such a pretty creature be anywhere, I believe.'

" ' I should be afraid he would get-hurt.'

" ' So I was, but the dog has sense enough; he gets into no danger, and keeps out of the way like a Christian.'

" 'May we go in, sir, and see Norman for a moment ?'

" ' Certainly,' Mr. Swift said; and himself led the way.

" Through several long rooms and rows of workers went Mr. Swift, and Mrs. Meadow and Silky after him, to the one where they found little Norman. He was standing before some sort of a machine, folding papers and pressing them against rows of pins, that were held all in order and with their points ready, by two pieces of iron in the machine. Norman was not working smartly, and looked already jaded, though it was early in the afternoon. Close at his feet, almost touching him, lay the little white dog. A very little and a most beautiful creature. Soft, white, curling hair, and large silky ears that drooped to the floor, as he lay with his head upon his

H

paws; and two gentle brown eyes looked almost pitifully up at the strangers. He did not get up; nor did Norman look round, till Mrs. Meadow spoke to him.

"'Hey, my boy, how are you getting on?' Mr. Swift said first, with a somewhat rough but not unkind slap across the shoulders. Norman shrugged his shoulders, and said,—

"'Pretty well, thank you, sir,—' when he heard Mrs. Meadow's soft, 'Norman, how do you do?'

"His fingers fell from the row of pin points, and he turned towards her, looking a good deal surprised and a little pleased, but with a very sober face.

"'Where have you been these two or three days?'

"'I've been here,' said Norman gravely.

"'How comes it you haven't been for Long-Ears' milk these days?

"'I—I couldn't,' said Norman.

"'Why?'

"'I hadn't any money—I gave it to mother.' He spoke low, and with some difficulty.

"'What made you do that, Norman?'

"He looked up at her.

"'Because,—you know,—Jesus said so.'

"Mrs. Meadow had been stooping down to

speak to him, but now she stood up straight, and for a minute she said nothing.

" ' And what has Long-Ears done, dear, without his milk ? '

" Norman was silent, and his mouth twitched. Mrs. Meadow looked at the little dog, which lay still where he had been when she came in, his gentle eyes having, she thought, a curious sort of wistfulness in their note-taking.

" · Won't he eat meat ? '

" Norman shook his head and said ' No,' under his breath.

" ' He's a dainty little rascal,' said the overseer; 'he was made to live on sweetmeats and sugarplums.' And Mr. Swift walked on.

" ' I've brought him some milk,' whispered Silky; and softly stooping down she uncovered her little tin-pail and tried to coax the dog to come to it. But Norman no sooner caught the words of her whisper and saw the pail, than his spirit gave way; he burst into a bitter fit of crying, and threw himself down on the floor and hid his face

" Mr. Swift came back to see what was the matter. Mrs. Meadow explained part to him, without telling of Norman's keeping the money.

" ' O well,' said Mr. Swift,—' but he mustn't

make such a disturbance about it—it's against all order ; and feeding the dog, too, Lois!—but it's a pretty creature. He's hungry, he is! Well ; it's well we don't have ladies come to the factory every day.'

" Silky's other name was Lois.

" ' I ll never do so again, Mr. Swift,' said she, gently.

" ' O I don't say that,' said he. ' I don't dislike the sight of you, Miss Lois ; but I must have you searched at the door. Keep this boy quiet, now, Mrs. Meadow ; and don't stay too long ; or take him with you.'

" The boy was quiet enough now. While Mr. Swift had been speaking he had raised himself from the floor, half up, and had stopped sobbing, and was looking at Long-Ears and gently touching his curly head ; who, on his part, was lapping the milk with an eagerness as if he had wanted it for some time. Norman's tears fell yet, but they fell quietly. By the time the little dog had finished the milk they did not fall at all. Till then nobody said anything.

" ' Come for it every morning again, my child,' said Mrs. Meadow, softly ;—' I 'll give it to you. What a dear little fellow he is! I don't wonder you love him. He shall have milk enough.'

" Norman looked up gratefully, and with a little bit of a smile.

" ' You don't look very strong, my boy,' said Mrs. Meadow. 'You don't feel right well, do you?'

" He shook his head, as if it was a matter beyond his understanding.

" ' Are you tired?'

" His eyes gave token of understanding that.

" ' Yes, I'm tired. People are not tired up there, are they?'

" ' Where, dear?'

" ' Up there—in heaven?'

" ' No, dear,' said Mrs. Meadow.

" ' I'll go there, won't I?'

" ' If you love Jesus and serve him, he will take good care of you and bring you safe there surely.'

" ' He will,' said Norman.

" ' But you're not going yet, I hope, dear,' said Mrs. Meadow, kissing him. 'Good bye. Come to-morrow, and you shall have the milk.'

" ' Will you read to me that again, some time?' he enquired wistfully.

" Mrs. Meadow could hardly answer. She and Silky walked back without saying three words to each other; and I never saw Mrs. Meadow

cry so much as she did that afternoon and
evening

" Norman came after that every morning for
the dog's milk; and many a Sunday he and Long-
Ears passed part of the time with Mrs. Meadow;
and many a reading he listened to there as he
had listened to the first one.   He didn't talk
much.   He was always near his little dog, and he
seemed quietly to enjoy everything at those
times.

" As the summer changed into autumn, and
autumn gave way to winter, Norman's little face
seemed to grow better looking, all the while it
was growing more pale and his little body more
slim.   It grew to be a contented, very quiet and
patient face, and his eye took a clearness and
openness it did not use to have; though he
never was a *bad*-looking child.   ' He won't live
long,' Mrs. Meadow said, after every Sunday.

" The little white dog all this while grew more
white and curly and bright-eyed every day; or
they all thought so.

" It was not till some time in January that at
last Norman stopped coming for milk, and did
not go by to the factory any more.   It was in a
severe bit of weather, when Mrs. Meadow was
shut up with a bad cold; and some days were

gone before she or Silky could get any news of him. Then, one cold evening, his mother came for milk, and to say that Norman was very ill and would like to see Lois and Mrs. Meadow. She was a miserable-looking woman, wretchedly dressed, and with a jaded, spiritless air, that seemed as if everything she cared for in life was gone, or she too poor to care for it. I thought Norman must have a sad home where she was. And his father must be much worse in another way, or his mother would not have such a look.

" Silky and Mrs. Meadow got ready directly. Silky put her purse in her pocket, as she generally did when she was going to see poor people, and wrapping up warm with cloaks and shawls and hoods, she and her mother set out. It was just sunset of a winter's day; clear enough, but uncommonly cold.

" ' It will be dark by the time we come home, mother,' said Silky.

" ' Yes, honey, but we can find the way,' came from under Mrs. Meadow's hood; and after that neither of them spoke a word.

" It was not a long way; they soon came to the edge of the town, and took a poor straggling street that ran where no good and comfortable buildings shewed themselves, or at least no good

and comfortable homes. Some of the houses
were decently well-built, but several families
lived in each of them, and comfort seemed to be
an unknown circumstance; at least after Mrs.
Meadow's nice kitchen, with the thick carpet, and
blazing fire, and dark cupboard doors, these all
looked so. The light grew dimmer and the air
grew colder, as Mrs. Meadow and Silky went
down the street; and Silky was trembling all
over by the time they stopped at one of these
brick dwelling-houses and went in.

"The front door stood open; nobody minded
that; it was nobody's business to shut it. They
went in, through a dirty entry, and up stairs that
nobody ever thought of cleaning, to the third
story. There Mrs. Meadow first knocked, and
then gently opened the door. A man was there,
sitting over the fire; a wretched tallow-light on
the table hardly shewed what he looked like. Mrs
Meadow spoke with her usual pleasantness.

"'Good evening, Mr. Finch. Can I see little
Norman?'

"'Yes,—I suppose so,' the man said, in a gruff
voice, and pointing to another door; 'they're in
yonder.'

"'How is he?'

"'I don't know!—Going, I expect.' He

spoke in a tone that might have been half heartless, half heartfull. Mrs. Meadow stayed no further questions. She left him there, and went on to the inner room.

" That was so dark, hardly anything could be seen. A woman rose up from some corner—it proved to be Mrs. Finch—and went for the light. Her husband's voice could be heard gruffly asking her what she wanted with it, and her muttered words of reply; and then she came back with it in her hand.

" The room was ill-lighted when the candle was in it, but there could be seen two beds; one raised on some sort of a bedstead, the other on the floor in a corner. No fire was in this room, and the bed was covered with all sorts of coverings; a torn quilt, an old great-coat, a small ragged worsted shawl, and Norman's own poor little jacket and trowsers. But on these, close within reach of the boy's hand, lay curled the little dog; his glossy white hair and soft outlines making a strange contrast with the rags and poverty and ugliness of the place.

" Norman did not look much changed, except that his face was so very pale it seemed as if he had no more blood to leave it. Mrs. Meadow and Silky came near, and neither of them at first was forward to speak. Mrs. Finch stood holding the light. Then Mrs. Meadow stooped down by the bed's head.

" ' Little Norman,' she said, and you could tell her heart was full of tears,—' do you know me ? '

" ' I know you,' he said, in a weak voice, and with a little bit of smile.

" ' How do you do ? '

" ' Very well,' he said, in the same manner.

" ' Are you very well ? ' said Mrs. Meadow.

" ' Yes,' he said. ' I 'm going now.'

" ' Where, dear ? '

" ' You know—to that good place. Jesus will take me, won't he ? '

" ' If you love and trust him, dear.'

" ' He will take me,' said Norman.

" ' What makes you think you 're going, dear ? ' said Mrs. Meadow.

" ' I can't stay,'—said Norman, shutting his eyes. He opened them again immediately. ' I 'm going,' he said. ' I 'm so tired. I sha'n't be tired there, shall I ? '

" ' No dear,' said Mrs. Meadow, whose power of speech was like to fail her. She kept wiping her face with her pocket-handkerchief. Norman stroked and stroked his little dog's silky head.

" ' Poor Long-Ears ! ' said he, faintly,—' poor

Long-Ears!—I can't take care of you now. Poor Long-Ears! you're hungry. He hasn't had anything to eat since—since—mother?'

" ' He don't know how time goes,' said Mrs. Finch, who had not before spoken. ' The dog hasn't had a sup of anything since day before yesterday. He has a right to be hungry. I don't know what he lives on. My husband don't care whether anything lives or not.'

" Silky had not said a word, and she didn't now, but she brought out that same little tin pail from under her cloak, and set it down on the floor. Norman's eye brightened. But the dog could not be coaxed to quit the bed; he would set only his two fore-feet on the floor, and so drank the milk out of the pail. Norman watched him, almost with a smile. And when the dog, having left the milk, curled himself down again in his old place, and looked into his master's face, Norman quite smiled.

" ' Poor Long-Ears!'—he said, patting him again with a feeble hand. ' I'm going to leave you,—what will you do?'

" ' I'll take care of him, Norman,' said Mrs. Meadow.

" ' Will you?' said Norman.

" ' As long as he lives, if you wish.'

" Norman signed for her to put her ear down
to him, and said earnestly,—

" ' I give him to you—you keep him. Will
you?'

" ' Yes, indeed, I will,' said Mrs. Meadow.

" ' Then you'll have milk enough, dear little
Long-Ears,' said Norman. ' But,' he said eagerly
to Mrs. Meadow, ' you must take him home with
you to-night—I'm afraid father will do something
with him if you don't.'

" ' But you will want him,' said Mrs. Meadow.

" ' No I won't. Father will do something
with him.'

" ' Indeed he will, sure enough,' said Mrs
Finch.

" ' Then I'll take him, and keep him, dear, as
if he was yourself,' said Mrs. Meadow.

" ' I won't want him,' said Norman, shutting
his eyes again ;—' I'm going.'

" ' And you're not sorry, dear?' said Mrs.
Meadow.

" ' No!' he said.

" ' I wonder why he should,' said Mrs. Finch,
wiping her eyes.

" ' And you know Jesus will take you?'

" ' Because I love him,' said Norman, without
opening his eyes.

" ' What makes you love him so, dear?'

" ' Because he did that for me,' said Norman, opening his eyes once more to look at her, and then re-shutting them. And he never opened them again. It seemed that having his mind easy about his pet, and having seen his friends, he wanted nothing more on this earth. He just slumbered away a few hours, and died so, as quietly as he had slept. His little pale meek face looked as if, as he said, he was glad to go.

" Nothing but a degree of force that no one would use could have moved Long-Ears from the body of his master, till it was laid in the grave. Then, with some difficulty, Mrs. Meadow gained possession of him, and brought him home."

" Is that all?" said Carl, when the story stopped.

" All."

" What more of Mrs. Meadow and Silky?"

" Nothing more. They lived there, and took care of Long-Ears, and were kind to everybody, and sold milk, just as they used."

" And what about Long-Ears?"

" Nothing about him. He lived there with Mrs. Meadow and Silky, and was as well off as a little dog could be."

And is that all?"

" That is all."

" And how did you get here?"

" I've told enough for once."

" I'll hear the rest another time," said Carl, as he grasped the purse, and ran off towards home; for it was getting to be high noon, and his mother had called to him that dinner was ready.

" Mother," said Carl, " I've heard the stories of my purse, and of my red cent, and of my three apples, and they're splendid!"

" What a child!" said Mrs. Krinken. " Are the stories not done yet?"

" No," said Carl; " and I don't know which to hear next. There's the boat, and the pine-cone, and the shoes, and the book, and the old stocking;—all of them;—and I don't know which to have first. Which would you, mother?"

" What's all that?" said John Krinken.

" He says his things tell him stories," said Mrs. Krinken; " and he's told over one or two to me, and it's as good as a book. I can't think where the child got hold of them."

" Why they *told* 'em to me, mother," said Carl.

" Yes," said Mrs. Krinken; " something told it to thee, child."

" Who told 'em, Carl?" said his father.

" My red cent, and my purse, and my three apples—or only one of the apples," said Carl ; —" that was Beachamwell."

" Beach 'em *what?*" said his father.

" Beachamwell—that is the biggest of my three apples," said Carl.

At which John and Mrs. Krinken looked at each other, and laughed till their eyes ran down with tears.

" Let's hear about Beachamwell," said John, when he could speak.

" I've told it," said Carl, a little put out.

" Yes ; and it was a pretty story, as ever I heard, or wish to hear," said Mrs. Krinken, soothingly.

" Let's hear the story of the shoes, then," said John.

" *I* haven't heard it yet," said Carl.

" O, and you can't tell it till you've heard it?" said his father.

" I haven't heard any of 'em but three," said Carl, " and I don't know which to hear next."

" The old stocking would tell you a rare story if it knew how," said his father; " it could spin you a yarn as long as its own."

" I'd rather hear the old pine-cone, John, '

said his wife. " Ask the pine-cone, Carl. I wish it could tell, and I hear !"

" Which first?" said Carl, looking from one to the other.

But John and Mrs. Krinken were too busy thinking of the story-teller to help him out with his question about the stories.

" Then I'm a going to keep the stocking for the very last one !" said Carl.

" Why?" said his mother.

" 'Cause it's ugly. And I guess I'll make the shoes tell me their story next; because I might want to put them on, you know !"

And Carl looked down at two sets of fresh-coloured toes, which looked out at him through the cracks of his old half-boots.

Mr. and Mrs. Krinken got up laughing, to attend to their business; and Carl indignantly seizing his shoes, ran off with them out of hearing to the sunny side of the house, where he plumped himself down on the ground with them in front of him, and commanded them to speak.

THE STORY OF THE TWO SHOES.

" I believe," said the right shoe, " that I am the first individual of my race whose history has ever been thought worth asking for.   I hope to improve my opportunity.   I consider it to be a duty in all classes for each member of the class——"

" You may skip about that," said Carl.   " I don't care about it."

" I am afraid," said the right shoe, " I am uninteresting. My excuse is, that I never was fitted to be anything else. Not to press upon people's notice is the very lesson we are especially learned; we were never intended to occupy a high position in society, and it is reckoned an unbearable fault in us to make much noise in the world."

" I say," said Carl, " you may skip that."

" I beg pardon," said the shoe, " I was coming to the point. ' Step by step' is our family motto.

I

However, I know young people like to get over the ground at a leap. I will do it at once.

" My brother and I are twins, and as much alike as it is possible perhaps for twins to be Mr. Peg, the cobbler, thought we were exactly alike; and our upper leathers did indeed run about on the same calf (as perchance they may another time), but our soles were once further apart than they are ever like to be for the future; one having roamed the green fields of Ohio on the back of a sturdy ox, while the other was raised in Vermont. However, we are mates now; and having been, as they say, ' cut out for each other,' I have no doubt we shall jog on together perfectly well.

" We are rather an old pair of shoes. In fact we have been on hand almost a year. I should judge from the remarks of our friend Mr. Peg when he was beginning upon us, that he was very unaccustomed to the trade of shoe-*making*— shoe-mending was what he had before lived by; or, perhaps, I should rather say, tried to live by; I am afraid it was hard work; and I suppose Mr. Peg acted upon the excellent saying, which is also a motto in our family, that ' It is good to have two strings to one's bow.' It was in a little light front room, looking upon the street, which was

"Hardly had Mr Pegg got the soles and the upper leathers and the vamps to his mind, and sat down on his chair to begin work, when a little girl came in."—P. 115.

Mr. Peg's parlour, and shop, and workroom, that he cut out the leather and prepared the soles for this his first manufacture. I think he hadn't stuff enough but for one pair, for I heard him sigh once or twice as he was fidgeting with his pattern over my brother's upper leather, till it was made out. Mr. Peg was a little oldish man, with a crown of grey hairs all round the back part of his head ; and he sat to work in his shirt sleeves, and with a thick, short leather apron before him. There was a little fire-place in the room, with sometimes fire in it, and sometimes not; and the only furniture was Mr. Peg's little bit of a counter, the low rush-bottomed chair in which he sat to work, and a better one for a customer ; his tools, and his chips—by which I mean the scraps of leather which he scattered about.

" Hardly had Mr. Peg got the soles and the upper leathers and the vamps to his mind, and sat down on his chair to begin work, when a little girl came in. She came from a door that opened upon a staircase leading to the upper room, and walked up to the cobbler. It was a little brown-haired girl, about nine or ten years old, in an old calico frock and pantalettes ; she was not becomingly dressed, and she did not look very well.

"'Father,' she said,—'mother's head aches again.'

"The cobbler paused in his work, and looked up at her.

"'And she wants you to come up and rub it—she says I can't do it hard enough.'

"Rather slowly Mr. Peg laid his upper leather and tools down.

"'Will you close this shoe for me, Sue, while I am gone?'

"He spoke half pleasantly, and half, to judge by his tone and manner, with some sorrowful meaning. So the little girl took it, for she answered a little sadly,—

"'I wish I could, father.'

"'I'm glad you can't, dear.'

"He laid his work down, and mounted the stairs. She went to the window, and stood with her elbows leaning on the sill, looking into the street.

"It is only a small town, that Beachhead; but still, being a sea-coast town, there is a good deal of stir about it. The fishermen from the one side, and the farmers from the other, with their various merchandise; the busy boys, and odd forms of women for ever bustling up and down, make it quite a lively place. There is always a good deal to see in the street. Yet the little girl stood very still and quiet by the window; her head did not turn this way and that; she stood like a stupid person, who did not know what was going on. A woman passing up the street stopped a moment at the window.

" ' How's your mother to-day, Sue?'

" ' She's getting along slowly, Mrs. Binch.'

" ' Does the doctor say she is dangerous any?'

" ' The doctor don't come any more.'

" ' Has he giv' her up!'

" ' Yes; he says there is nothing to do but to let her get well.'

" ' O!—she's so smart, is she?'

" ' No, ma'am,—she's not smart at all: he says ——'

" But Mrs. Binch had passed on, and was out of hearing; and the little brown head stood still at the window again, leaning now on one hand. It was a smooth-brushed, round little head, seen against the open window. By and by another stopped, a lady this time; a lady dressed in black. with a grave, sweet, delicate face.

" ' How's your mother, Sue?'

" ' She's just the same way, Mrs. Lucy.'

" ' No better?'

" ' Not much, ma'am. It'll take a long time, the doctor says.'

" ' And are you, poor little tot, all alone in the house to do everything ? '

" ' No, ma'am ;—there 's father.'

" The sweet face gave her a sort of long, wistful look, and passed on. Sue stood there yet at the window, with her head leaning on her hand ; and whatever was the reason, so dull of hearing that her father had come down, seated himself in his work-chair, and taken up his shoe, several minutes before she found it out. Then she left the window and came to him.

" ' What shall I do, father ? '

" ' She 'll want you directly,' said the cobbler ' She 's asleep now.'

" Sue stood still.

" ' Don't you want some dinner, Sue ? '

" She hesitated a little, and then said ' yes.'

" ' Well, see, dear, and make some more of that porridge. Can you ? '

" ' Yes, father ; there 's some meal yet. And there 's some bread, too.'

" ' You may have that,' said the cobbler. ' And I 'll go out by and by, and see if I can get a little money. Mr. Shipham had a pair of boots new soled a month ago ; and Mr. Binch owes me for some jobs — if I ever could get hold of them.'

" And the cobbler sighed.

" 'If people only knew, they would pay you, father, wouldn't they?'

" 'There is one that knows,' said the cobbler ' And why they don't pay me he knows. Maybe it's to teach you and me, Sue, that man does not live by bread alone.'

" ' But by every word that proceedeth out of the mouth of God doth man live,' his little daughter went on softly, as if she were filling up the words for her own satisfaction. ' But didn't we know that before, father ?'

" 'Maybe we didn't know it enough,' said the cobbler. ' I'm afraid I don't now.'

" And as her back was turned, he hastily brought his hand to his eyes.

" 'But father, can one help feeling a little bad when—when things are so now?'

" ' 'A little bad'— perhaps one might feel ' *a little bad*,' said the cobbler ; ' but if I believed all that I know, I don't see how I could feel *very* bad. I don't see how I could ; and I oughtn't to.'

" His little daughter had been raking the fire together, and setting on the coals a little iron skillet of water. She turned and looked at him when he said this, as if she had not known before

that he did feel 'very bad.' 'He did not see the
look, which was a startled and sorrowful one ; he
was bending over his shoe-leather. She left the
room then and went after the meal, which she
brought in a yellow earthen dish, and began
silently to mix for the porridge.

" ' The Bible says, father——' she began, stirring away.

" ' Yes, dear,—what does it say?' said Mr. Peg

" 'It says, '*Trust in the Lord and do good;
so shalt thou dwell in the land, and verily*——''

" Susan's voice broke. She stirred her por
ridge vehemently, and turned her back to her
father.

" ' '*Verily thou shalt be fed*,' ' said the cobbler.
'Yes—I know it. The thing is, to believe it.'

" ' You do believe it, father,' Susan said,
softly.

" ' Ay, but I haven't trusted the Lord, nor
done good, any to speak of. It'll stand good
for you, daughter, if it doesn't for me.'

" She had stirred her meal into the skillet;
and now, setting down her dish, she came to his
side, and putting her two arms round his neck,
she kissed him all over his face. The cobbler let
fall leather and ends, and hugged her up to his
breast.

" ' That's done me more good than dinner now,' said he, when he had, albeit tearfully, given her two or three sound kisses by way of finishing. ' You may have all the porridge, Susie.'

" ' There's enough, father; and there's some bread, too.'

" ' Eat it all up,' said the cobbler, turning to his work again, maybe to hide his eyes. She stood leaning on his shoulder, just so as not to hinder the play of his arm.

" ' Shall I keep the bread for supper, father ? '

" ' No, dear; maybe I'll get some money before supper.'

" ' Whose shoes are those, father ? '

" ' They aren't anybody's yet.'

" ' Whose are they going to be ? '

" ' I don't know.—The first pair of feet that come along that will fit 'em. If I sell these I'll get some leather and make more.'

" ' Is that the last of your leather, father ? '

" ' Ay—the last big enough; the rest is all pieces.'

" She stood a little while longer, laying her head on his shoulder; then came a knocking up stairs, and she ran away. The cobbler wrought at his shoe for a space, when turning his head, he dropped everything to go and see after the por-

ridge; and he squatted over the fire, stirring it,
till such time as he thought it was done, and he
drew back the skillet. He went to the foot of
the stairs, and looked up and listened for a
minute, and then left it and came back without
calling anybody. It was plain he must eat his
dinner alone.

" His dinner was nothing but porridge and salt,
eaten with what would have been a good appetite
if it had had good thoughts to back it. And the cobbler did not seem uncheerful; only once or twice
he stopped and looked a good while with a grave
face into the fire or on the hearth. But a porridge dinner after all could not last long. Mr.
Peg set away his plate and spoon, placed the
skillet carefully in the corner of the fire-place,
took off his leather apron, and put on his coat;
and, taking his hat from the counter, he went
out.

" There were no more stitches set in the shoe
that afternoon, for Mr. Peg did not get home till
dark. The first thing that happened after he
went away, a gust of wind blew round the house
and came down the chimney, bringing with it a
shower of soot, which must have sprinkled pretty
thick upon the open skillet. Then the wind
seemed to go up chimney again, and could be

heard whistling off among the neighbouring housetops. A while after, little Susie came down, and made for her skillet. She pulled it out, and fetched her plate and spoon, and began to skim out the soot. But I suppose she found it pretty bad, or else that it would lose her a good deal of the porridge; for one time she set her plate and spoon down on the hearth beside her, and laid her face in her apron. She soon took it up again; but she didn't make a large meal of the porridge.

"She went up-stairs then immediately, and when she came down the second time it was near evening. She stood and looked about to see that her father was not come in; then she built up the fire, and when it was burning stood and looked into it, just in the same way that she had stood and looked out of the window. Suddenly she wheeled about, and coming behind the counter took her father's Bible from a heap of bits of leather where it lay, and went and sat down on the hearth with it; and as long as there was light to see, she was bending over it. Then, when the light faded, she clasped her hands upon the shut Bible, and leaning back against the jamb fell fast asleep in an instant, with her head against the stone

" There she was when her father came home. Her feet were stretched out upon the hearth, and he stumbled over them. That waked her. By the glimmering light of the embers something could be seen hanging from Mr. Peg's hand.

" 'Have you got home, father?—I believe I got asleep waiting for you. What have you got in your hand?—Fish!—Oh, father!—'

" You should have heard the change of little Sue's voice when she spoke that. Generally her way of speaking was low and gentle like the twilight, but those two words were like a burst of sunshine.

" 'Yes, dear—Blow up the fire, so you can see them—I've been to Mrs. Binch's—I've been all over town, a'most—and Mrs. Binch's boy had just come in with some, and she gave me a fine string of 'em—nice blue fish—there.'

" Susan had made a light blaze, and then she and the cobbler admired and turned and almost *smelt* of the fish, for joy.

" 'And shall we have one for supper, father?'

" 'Yes dear—You have some coals and I'll get the fish ready right off. Has mother had all she wanted to-day?'

" 'Yes, father—Mrs. Lucy sent her some soup, and she had plenty. And I saved the bread from dinner, father, isn't it good; and there's more porridge too.'

" What a bed of coals Sue had made, by the time her father came back with the fish, nicely cleaned and washed. She put it down, and then the two sat over it in the firelight and watched it broil. It was done as nicely as a fish could be done; and Susan fetched the plates, and the salt, and the bread; and then the cobbler gave thanks to God for their supper. And then the two made such a meal! there wasn't a bone of that fish but was clean picked, nor a grain of salt but what did duty on a sweet morsel. There was not a scrap of bread left from that supper; and I was as glad as anything of my tough nature can be, to know that there were several more fish beside the one eaten. Sue cleared away the things when they had done, ran up to see if her mother was comfortable, and soon ran down again. Her step had changed too.

" 'Now darling,' said her father, 'come and let us have our talk by this good firelight.'

" She came to his arms and kissed him; and his arms were wrapped round her, and she sat on his knee.

" 'It's one good thing, you haven't lights to

work, so we can talk,' said Sue, stroking his face
' If you had, we couldn't.'

" 'Maybe we would,' said the cobbler. ' Let
us talk to-night of the things we have to be
thankful for.'

" ' There's a great many of them, father,' said
Sue, with her twilight voice.

" ' The first thing is, that we know we have a
Friend in heaven ; and that we do love and trust
him.'

" ' O father ! ' said Sue,—' if you begin with
that, all the other things will not seem anything
at all.'

" ' That's true,' said Mr. Peg. ' Well, Sue,
let 's have 'em all. You begin.'

" ' I don't know what to begin with,' said Sue,
looking into the fire.

" ' I have you,' said her father, softly kissing
her.

" ' O father !—and I have you ;—but now you
are taking the next best things.'

" ' I shouldn't care for all the rest without this
one,' said the cobbler ;—' nor I shouldn't mind
anything but for this,' he added, in a somewhat
changed tone.

" ' But father, you mustn't talk of that to-

night ;—we are only going to talk of the things
we have to be thankful for.'

" ' Well, we'll take the others to-morrow night,
maybe, and see what we can make of them.   Go
on, Susie,' said the cobbler, putting his head
down to her cheek,—' I have my dear little child,
and she has her father.   That's something to
thank God and to be glad for,—every day.'

" ' So I do, every day, father,' said Susan very
softly.

" ' And so do I,' said the cobbler; ' and while
I can take care of thee, my dearest, I will take
trouble for nothing else.'

" ' Now you are getting upon the other things,
father,' said Sue.   ' Father, it is something to be
thankful for that we can have such a nice fire
every night,—and every day, if we want it.'

" ' You don't know what a blessing 'tis, Sue,'
said her father.   ' If we lived where we couldn't
get drift-wood,—if we lived as some of the poor
people do in the great cities, without anything
but a few handfuls of stuff to burn in the hardest
weather, and that wretched stuff for making a fire,
—I am glad you don't know how good it is, Sue!'
said he, hugging his arms round her.   ' There
isn't a morning of my life but I thank God for
giving us wood, when I go about kindling it.'

" ' How do they do in those places, without wood?' said Sue, sticking out her feet towards the warm, ruddy blaze.

" ' He who knows all only knows,' said the cobbler, gravely. ' They do without! It seems to me I would rather go without eating, and have a fire.'

" ' I don't know,' said Sue thoughtfully, ' which I would rather. But those poor people haven't either, have they?'

" ' Not enough,' said the cobbler. ' They manage to pick up enough to keep them alive somehow.'—And he sighed, for the subject came near home.

" ' Father,' said Sue, ' I don't believe God will let us starve.'

" ' I do not think he will, my dear,' said the cobbler.

" ' Then why do you sigh?'

" ' Because I deserve that he should, I believe,' said the cobbler, hanging his head. ' I deserve it, for not trusting him better. ' *Casting all your care upon him, for he careth for you.*' Ah, my dear, we can't get along without running to our upper storehouse pretty often.'

" ' Father, I guess God don't mean we should.'

" ' That 's just it!' said the cobbler. ' That is

just, no doubt, what he means. Well dear, let's learn the lesson he sets us.'

" ' Then, father,' said Sue, ' don't you think we have a good little house? It's large enough, and it's warm.'

" ' Yes dear,' said the cobbler·; some of those poor people we were talking about would think themselves as well off as kings if they had such a house to live in as this '

" ' And it is in a pleasant place, father, where there are a great many kind people.'

" ' I hope there are,' said the cobbler, who was thinking at the moment how Mr. Shipham had put him off, and Mr. Dill had dodged him, and Mr. Binch had fought every one of his moderate charges

" ' Why, father!' said Sue, ' there's Mrs. Lucy every day sends things to mother; and Mrs. Binch gave you the fish; and Mrs. Jackson came and washed ever so many times ; and—and Mrs. Gelatin sent the pudding and other things for mother, you know.'

" ' Well, dear,' said the cobbler,—' yes,—it seems that woman-kind is more plenty here, at any rate, than man-kind.

" ' Why, father ?' said Sue

K

" 'I hope you'll never know, dear,' he answered. 'It was a foolish speech of mine.'

" 'And I'm sure it's a blessing, father, that we have so many things sent us for mother,—she has almost as much as she wants, and things we couldn't get. Now, Mrs. Lucy's soup,—you don't know how nice it was. I tasted just the least drop in the spoon; and mother had enough of it for to-day and to-morrow. And then the doctor says she'll get well by and by; and that will be a blessing.'

" It was a blessing so far off, that both the cobbler and his little daughter looked grave as they thought about it.

" 'And I'm well, father, and you're well,' said Sue, pleasantly.

" 'Thank God!' said the cobbler.

" 'And father, don't you think it's a little blessing to live near the sea? and to have the beautiful beach to walk upon, and see the waves come tumbling in, and smell the fresh wind? We used to go so often, and maybe by and by we shall again Don't you think it is a great deal pleasanter than it would be if Beachhead was away off in the country, out of sight of the water?'

" ' Ah, Sue,' said her father,—' I don't know ;—
I've lived a good piece of my life in one of those
in-shore places, and I didn't want to hear the sea
roar then-a-days, and I could get along without
the smell of salt water. No,—you don't know
what you are talking about exactly ; every sort of
place that the Lord has made has its own pretti-
ness and pleasantness ; and so the sea has ; but I
love the green pasture-fields as well as I do the
green field of water, to this day.'

" ' But one might be in a place where there
wasn't the sea nor the pasture-fields either,
father.'

" ' So one might,' said the cobbler. ' Yes,
there are plenty such places. The sea *is* a blessing. I was thinking of my old home in Connec-
ticut ; but the world isn't all green hills and sea-
shore,—there's something else in it—something
else. Yes, dear, I love those big waves, too.'

" ' And then, father,' said Sue, laying her
hand on his breast, ' we come back to the best
things,—that you were beginning with.'

" ' Ay,' said the cobbler, clasping his arm round
her ; and for a little space they sat silent and
looked into the fire,—and then he went on.

" ' Poor as we sit here, and weak and dying as

we know we are, we know that we have a taber
nacle on high,—a house not made with hands,
eternal in the heavens.   It won't matter much,
Sue, when we get there—'

" *What* would not matter the cobbler did not
say ; there was something came in his throat that
stopped him.

" ' It won't matter, father,' said Sue, softly.

" They sat still a good little while ; the flame
of the bits of brands in the chimney leaped up
and down, burned strong and then fell outright ;
and the red coals glowed and glimmered in the
place of it, but with less and less power.

" ' Now, Sue, let's read,' said the cobbler on a
sudden

" She got up, and he put on the coals two or
three pieces of light stuff, which soon blazed up.
While he was doing this, Sue brought the Bible.
Then she took her former place in her father's
arms ; and he opened the book and read by the
firelight, pausing at almost every sentence,—

" ' ' *Praise ye the Lord* '—We will do that,
Sue,' said the cobbler,—' for ever.'

" ' ' *Blessed is the man that feareth the Lord
that delighteth greatly in his commandments.*' '

" ' You do that, father,' said Sue, softly.

" ' I do fear him; I do delight in his commandments,' said the poor cobbler. ' I might a
great deal more. But see how it goes on.'

" ' ' *His seed shall be mighty upon earth; the
generation of the upright shall be blessed.*' No
doubt of it: only let us see that we are upright,
my child.'

" ' ' *Wealth and riches shall be in his house.*'
So they are, Sue; aren't we rich?'

" ' Yes father. But don't you think that
means the other kind of riches, too?'

" ' I don't know,' said the cobbler; ' if it
does, we shall have them. But I don't know,
daughter; see,—

" ' ' *Wealth and riches shall be in his house;
and his righteousness endureth for ever.*' It seems
as if that riches had to do with that righteousness.
You know what Jesus says,—' *I counsel thee to
buy of me gold tried in the fire, that thou mayest be
rich.*' I guess it is the kind of riches of that man
who is described ' as having nothing, and yet
possessing all things.''

" ' Well, so we do, father: don't we?'

" ' Let us praise him,' said the cobbler.

" ' *Unto the upright there ariseth light in the
darkness.*' What a promise!'

" ' Unto the *upright*, again,' said Sue.

" ' Mind it, dear Sue,' said her father ; ' for we may see darker times than we have seen yet.'

" Sue looked úp at him gravely, but did not speak.

" ' ' *Unto the upright there ariseth light in the darkness: he is gracious, and full of compassion, and righteous.*' '

" ' That is, the upright man,' said Sue.

" ' ' *A good man showeth favour and lendeth: he will guide his affairs with discretion. Surely he shall not be moved for ever: the righteous shall be in everlasting remembrance.*' You remember who says, ' *I have graven thee upon the palms of my hands; thy walls are continually before me.*' '

" ' That is Zion, father, isn't it ? ' said Sue.

" ' And just before that,—' *Can a woman forget her sucking child, that she should not have compassion on the son of her womb? Yea, they may forget, yet will I not forget thee.*' '

" ' We oughtn't to be afraid, father,' said Sue, softly.

" ' I am not afraid,' said the cobbler.

" ' ' *The righteous shall be in everlasting remembrance. He shall not be afraid of evil tidings; his heart is fixed, trusting in the Lord.*'—There it is, Sue.'

" ' ' *His heart is established; he shall not be*

*afraid, until he see his desire upon his enemies. He
hath dispersed, he hath given to the poor; his righteousness endureth for ever; his horn shall be exalted
with honour. The wicked shall see it, and be
grieved; he shall gnash with his teeth and melt
away; the desire of the wicked shall perish.''*

" The cobbler closed the book; and he and his
little daughter knelt down, and he prayed for a
few minutes; then they covered up the fire, and
they went away up-stairs together. And the night
was as quiet in that house as in any house in the
land.

" The next morning the cobbler and his daughter broiled another fish; but the breakfast was a
shorter and less talkative affair than the supper
had been. After breakfast the cobbler sat down
to his work; but before the shoe was half an hour
nearer to being done, Sue appeared at the bottom
of the stairs with,—

" ' Father, mother says she wants a piece of
one of those fish.'

" The cobbler's needle stood still.

" ' I don't believe it is good for her,' said he.

" ' She says she wants it.'

" ' Well, can't you put it down, my daughter?

" ' Yes, father; but she says she wants me to

put her room up, and she's in a great hurry for the fish.'

" Mr. Peg slowly laid his work down. Sue ran up-stairs again, and the cobbler spent another half-hour over the coals and a quarter of a blue fish. Sue came for it, and the cobbler returned to his work again.

" It was a pretty cold day; the wind whistled about and brought the cold in; and every now and then Sue came down and stood at the fire a minute to warm herself. Every time the cobbler stayed his hand and looked up, and looked wistfully at her.

" ' Never mind, father,' said Sue. ' It's only that I am a little cold '

" ' You're blue,' said he.

" And at last Mr. Peg couldn't stand it. Down went the leather one side of him, and the tools the other; and he went and lugged an armful or two of sticks up-stairs, and built a fire there, in spite of Sue's begging him to keep on with his work and not mind her.

" ' But we sha'n't have wood enough, father,' she said at last gently.

" ' I'll go o'nights to the beach, and fetch a double quantity,' said the cobbler ;—' till your mo-

ther is able to come down-stairs. *That* I can do.
I can't bear the other thing, if you can.'

"And Sue stayed up - stairs, and the cobbler
wrought after that pretty steadily for some hours.
But in the middle of the afternoon came a new
interruption. Two men came into the shop, and
gave an order or two to the cobbler, who served
them with unusual gravity.

" ' When is Court-day, Sheriff?' he asked, in
the course of business.

" ' To-morrow itself, Mr. Peg.'

" ' To-morrow !' said the cobbler.

" ' What's the matter ? Comes the wrong day ?
It always does.'

" ' I had forgot all about it,' said the cobbler.
' Can't I be let off, sir ?'

" ' From what ?' said the other man.

" ' Why, it's rather an ugly job, some think,'
returned the sheriff. ' He's got to sit on the
jury that is to try Simon Ruffin.'

" ' I must beg to be let off,' said the cobbler,
' I am not at all able to leave home.'

" ' You must tell the court, then,' said he who
was called the sheriff; ' but it won't do any good,
I don't believe   Everybody says the same thing,
pretty much ; they don't any of 'em like the job;
but you see, this is a very difficult and important

case; a great many have been thrown out; it is
hard to get just the right men, those that are
altogether unobjectionable; and every one knows
you, Mr. Peg.'

" ' But my family want me,' said the cobbler;
' they can't do without me at home. Can't you
let me go, Mr. Packum ?'

" ' Not I,' said the sheriff; ' that's no part of my
privilege : you must ask the court, Mr. Peg.'

" ' To-morrow ?' said the cobbler.

" ' Yes, to-morrow ; but I tell you beforehand
it won't do any good. What excuse can you
make ?'

" ' My family want my care,' said the poor cobbler.

" ' So does every man's family,' said the sheriff,
with a laugh ; ' he's a happy man that don't find
it so. You haven't much of a family, Mr. Peg,
have you ?—if you had my seven daughters to
look after —— Well, Mr. Jibbs, — shall we
go ?'

" They went ; and sitting down again in his
chair the poor cobbler neglected his work, and
bent over it with his head in his hand. At length
he got up, put his work away, and left the room.
For a while his saw might be heard going at the
back of the house ; then it ceased, and nothing at

all was to be heard for a long time; only a light footstep overhead now and then. The afternoon passed, and the evening came.

" The cobbler was the first to make his appearance. He came in, lighted the fire which had quite died out, and sat down as he had sat before, with his head in his hand. So his little daughter found him. She stepped lightly and he did not hear her till her hand was on his shoulder. Then she asked him what was the matter?

" 'Oh!—nothing that should make me sit so,' said the cobbler, rousing himself.

" 'We've got more fish left yet,' said Sue.

" 'Yes, dear,—'tisn't that; but I've got to go away to-morrow '

" 'Away!' said Sue.

" 'Yes, away to court.'

" 'What for, father?'

" 'Why, they've got me down for a juryman, and I'm afraid there'll be no getting off. The sheriff says there won't.'

" 'What have you got to do, father?'

" 'Sit on a jury, dear, to decide whether Simon Ruffin is guilty or no.'

" 'Simon Ruffin! —that shot that man!—Oh, father!'

" 'It's pretty bad ' said the cobbler.

" ' How long will you be gone?'

" ' I can't tell at all,' said the cobbler; ' maybe a day—a day! they can't take the evidence in two days. I don't know whether it will be two or three days, or a week, dear.'

" ' A week—And what shall we do?' Sue could not help saying.

" ' If I can get off, I will,' said the cobbler; ' but in case I can't, I have or I will have by morning, as much wood as will do till I come back. I have two-and-sixpence besides, which I can leave you, darling; and I can do nothing more but trust.'

" ' Father, isn't it hard to trust sometimes?' Sue said with her eyes full of tears. The poor cobbler wrapped her in his arms and kissed them away, but he did not try to answer.

" ' Maybe it won't do us any harm after all,' said Sue more brightly;—' or maybe you will be able to come back, father. Father, you know we are to talk over to-night the things that we have that we can't be thankful for.'

" ' ' *In everything give thanks,* ' ' said the cobbler.

" ' Yes, father, but it doesn't say *for* everything.

" ' Perhaps not,' said the cobbler. ' Well, darling, we'll see. Let's have our supper first.'

" ' We'll have the biggest fish to-night, father.'

" The fish wasn't just out of the water now, but it was eaten with a good will; not quite so cheerily as the first one the night before; and Sue sighed once or twice as she was putting the dishes away, and didn't step quite so lightly. Then she came to her former place in her father's arms, and her head stooped upon his shoulder, and his cheek was laid to her forehead, and so they sat some minutes without speaking.

" ' Come, father,' said Sue,—' will you talk ?'

" ' Yes, dear. Let us tell over what we have to bear, and see how we can bear it.'

" ' We must go to our ' upper storehouse ' again for that, father.'

" ' Ay, dear,—always.'

" ' The first thing, I suppose,' said Sue, ' is that we haven't quite money enough.'

" ' We have just what God gives us,' said the cobbler. ' I'll never complain of that.'

" ' Why you never complain of anything, father. But it isn't pleasant.'

" ' No, dear,' said the cobbler ;—' and yet if we had money enough, could we trust God as we do? It is a sweet thing to live at his hand directly; to feel that it is feeding us to-day, and to know that it will to-morrow; for, ' was he ever a wil-

derness to Israel?' No, dear; I don't mean to
say that poverty is not hard to bear sometimes;
nor I don't mean to say that I wouldn't give you
plenty of everything if I had it to give; but I do
say that there is a sweet side even to this.'

" 'Father, our blue fish wouldn't have tasted
as good if we had always had plenty of them.'

" 'I suppose not,' said the cobbler, with a
little bit of a stifled sigh;—'and maybe we
shouldn't know how to love each other quite so
well, Sue '

" 'O, yes we should!' said Sue.

" 'I don't know,' said the cobbler. 'I
shouldn't know what my little daughter can do,
and bear, if she had not had a chance to shew
me.'

" 'Why I don't have much to bear, father,
said Sue

" 'Mother wouldn't know what a good nurse
you can be.

" 'I wish she hadn't a chance to know that,
father.'

" 'Yes,' said the cobbler,—'your mother's sick-
ness—that seems the hardest evil we have had to
do with. It's not easy to find any present comfort of that; nor any present good; for I am
afraid it makes me more impatient than patient.

Maybe that's why I have it.   But if we can't see
the reason of a great many things now, we shall
by and by.   We shall know, Sue, what the reason was.   *'Thou shalt remember all the way
which the Lord thy God led thee these forty years
in the wilderness, to humble thee and to prove thee,
to know what was in thine heart, whether thou
wouldest keep his commandments or no.'*"

"Sue lifted up her head, and her little face
was beautiful for the strong patience, and bright
trust, and love that was in it.   Her eyes were
swimming and her lips were speaking, though
they only moved to tremble.

" 'We can wait, Sue,' said the cobbler, gently.
Sue laid down her head again.

" ' So it seems we have got the reason of it
already,' Mr. Peg went on, ' if not the good.'

" 'Maybe we've got some of the good too,
without knowing it,' said his little daughter.

" ' Still, we'll be very glad to have mother get
well.'

" ' Oh, won't we !' said Sue.

" ' And it will teach us how to be thankful for
the common things we forget.'

" There was a little pause.

" ' Then you would like to have me go to
school,' said Sue ; ' and I can't.'

" 'And if you could I shouldn't have the plea
sure of teaching you myself,' said the cobbler.
'I can bear that.'

" 'But then I can't learn so many things,'
said Sue

" 'Of one kind you can't, and of another kind
you can,' said her father 'I don't believe there's
a school-girl in Beachhead that can broil a blue
fish as you can.'

" 'O father! — but then you shewed me
how.'

" ' Do you think broiling blue fish comes by
nature?' said the cobbler. 'I can tell you there
are many people that can't learn it at all. And
that's only one of your accomplishments.'

" 'O father!' said Sue again, smiling a
little.

" 'You can nurse a sick mother, and mend a
hole in your father's coat, and put up a room,
and make a bed, with anybody.'

" ' Still, father, you'd like to have me go ?'

" ' Yes, I would,' said the cobbler. 'Maybe 1
shall never be sorry, by and by, that I couldn't.'

" 'And then, father,' said Sue, ' you can't get
work enough.'

" ' Yes!' said the cobbler. 'If I could do that,
it would be all smooth. But God could give it to

me if it pleased him, and if it don't please him
there must be some reason ; can't we trust him
and wait?'

" Sue looked up again, not so brightly as once
before ; meekly, and rather tearfully.

" ' And then I must leave you to-morrow,' said
her father, kissing her brow ;—' that seems just
now the worst of all.'

" ' Maybe you'll come back again, father,' said
Sue.

" ' I am afraid I shall not—till this trial is
over.'

" ' It's a disagreeable business ; isn't it, father?'

" ' Very disagreeable—as ugly as can be to
look at.'

" They were silent awhile.

" ' Maybe there'll some good come of it, somehow, after all,' said Sue, in her twilight voice.

" ' Good will be the end of it,' said the cobbler.
'There's a kind hand doing it, and an almighty arm
upholding us in it; we shall not be utterly cast
down : so we must bear to be poor, and to be sick,
and to be separated; and just leave it all with
God.'

" ' Father, it's pleasant to do that,' said Sue ;
but you could know by the tone of her words that
she was crying a little

L

" ' Why, darling, if we *are* poor, and sick, and
in trouble, we have our dear Saviour, and we
know that the Lord is our God. We are not poor
people,— not we. ' Having nothing, and yet
possessing all things.' Who would we change
with, Sue ?'

" She had to wait a little while before she
spoke, but then she said,—

" ' I wouldn't change with anybody.'

" ' No more would I,' said the cobbler, giving
her another kiss.

" And so they went to bed, a couple of very
rich poor people.

" But the house looked poor the next day;
empty and cold. The cobbler was off betimes;
the little breakfast-fire died out; dust lay on
the counter; the tools and the unfinished work
were here and there; the wind slipped in and
slipped out again; and nothing else paid us a
visit, except Sue, who once or twice looked in
and looked round, as if to see whether her father
. were there. Once she came into the room and
stood a few minutes, with her little brown head
and quiet grave face, looking at the ashes in the
fire-place, and the neglected work, and her father's
chair, with a wistful sort of eye. It said, or
seemed to say, that however she felt last night,

she would be very glad to-day if they were not poor, nor sick, nor separated. She looked pale and weary, too; but she did not stay long to rest or think. Her feet could be heard now and then up stairs. The cobbler did not come home; the night darkened upon just such an afternoon as the morning had been.

"The next day began in the same manner. Towards noon, however, the outer door opened, and in came a puff of fresh cold air, and another visiter, who looked fresh, but not cold at all. It was a boy about thirteen or fourteen; healthy, ruddy, bright-eyed, well-dressed, and exceeding neat in his dress. He came in like one familiar with the place, and took note of all the unusual tokens about, as if he knew well what was usual and what was unusual. He looked at the cold chimney and scattered work; he went to the foot of the stairs and stood listening a moment; and then coming away from there, he loitered about the room, now going to the window and now to the chimney, evidently waiting. He had to wait a good while, but he waited. At last he had what he wanted; for, tired with being up-stairs, or wanting to gather some news from the outer world, Sue slowly came down the stairs and shewed her little face at the stairway door. And

almost before it had time to change, the new-
comer had called out,—

" ' Sue ! '—

" And with an unknown light breaking all over
her face, Sue exclaimed, joyously, 'Roswald !—'
and springing across to him, laid her sweet lips
to his with right good will.

" ' O you've got back ! ' said Sue, with a glad-
someness it did, or would have done, any one's
heart good to hear.

" ' Here I am.   Haven't I been a long while
away ? '

" ' O so long ! ' said Sue

" ' But what's the matter here, Sue ? what's
become of you all ? '

" ' Why mother's sick, you know,—she hasn't
got well yet; and father's away.'

" ' Where is he ? '

" ' He had to go to court—he had to be a jury
man, to try Simon Ruffin.'

" ' When ? '

" ' Yesterday morning. And we hoped he would
be able to get leave to come away, we wanted him
so much ; but he hasn't been able to come.' '

" ' He's been away since yesterday morning.
Who's taking care of you ? '

" ' Why, nobody,' said Sue.

" ' Is there nobody in the house with you?'

" ' Nobody but mother. Father left wood enough all ready.'

" ' Wood enough for how long?'

" ' O for a good many days.'

" ' Aren't you afraid?'

" ' Why, no, Roswald!'

" ' Who goes to market for you, Sue?'

" ' Nobody.'

" ' What do you live on?'

" ' Oh, people send mother nice things—Mrs. Lucy sent her a whole pail of soup the other day.'

" ' How big a pail?'

" ' Why, Roswald!—I mean a nice little tin pail, so big.'

" ' And do you live on soup too?'

" ' No,' said Sue.

" ' On what, then?'

" ' O on what there is.'

" ' Exactly. And what is there?'

" ' Mrs. Binch gave father a string of blue fish the other night; and since then I have made porridge.'

" ' What sort of porridge?'

" ' Corn-meal porridge.'

" ' Why, Sue!—do you live on that?'

" ' Why, porridge is very good,' said Sue, looking at him. But there was a change in his eye,
and there came a glistening in hers; and then
she threw suddenly her two arms round his neck
and burst into a great fit of crying.

" If Roswald had been a man, his arm could
not have been put round her with an air of more
manly and grave support and protection; and
there were even one or two furtive kisses, as if
between boyish pride and affection : but affection
carried it.

" ' I don't know what made me cry,' said Sue,
at last, rousing herself; after she had had her cry
out.

" ' Don't you?' said Roswald.

" ' No. It couldn't have been these things;
because father and I were talking about them the
other night, and we agreed that we didn't feel
poor at all; at least, of course we felt poor, but
we felt rich, too.'

" ' How long have you been living on porridge?'

" ' I don't know. Have you had a fine time,
Roswald?'

" ' Yes, very. I'll tell you all about it some
time, but not now.'

" ' Is Merrytown as pleasant as Beachhead?'

" ' It is more pleasant.'

" 'More pleasant!' said Sue. 'Without the beach, and the waves, Roswald!'

" 'Yes, it is; and you'd say so, too. You'd like it better than anybody. There are other things there instead of beach and waves. You shall go down there some time, Sue, and see it.'

" 'I can't go,' said Sue meekly.

" 'Not now, but some day. Sue, haven't you any money?'

" 'I've two-and-sixpence, that father gave me; but I was afraid to spend any of it, for fear he or mother might want it for something. I must, though, for I haven't got but a very little Indian meal.'

" 'Sue, have you had dinner to-day?'

" 'Not yet. I was just coming down to see about it.'

" 'Your mother don't eat porridge, does she?'

" 'O no. She's had her dinner.'

" 'Well, will you let me come and eat dinner with you?'

" Sue brought her hands together, with again a flush of great joy upon her face; and then put them in both his.

" 'How good it is you have got back!' she said.

" 'It will take that porridge a little while to

get ready, won't it?' said he, beating her hands gently together, and looking as bright as a button.

" ' O yes—it'll take a little while,' said Sue. ' I haven't got the water boiling yet.'

" ' Have you got meal enough for both of us?'

" ' Yes, I guess so ;—plenty.'

" Just then Mrs. Lucy opened the front door and brought her sweet face into the room. She looked a little hard at the two children, and asked Sue how her mother was. Roswald bowed, and Sue answered

" ' May I go up and see her?'

" Sue gave permission. Mrs. Lucy went up the stairs. Roswald stopped Sue as she was following.

" ' Sue, I'll go to market for you to-day. Give me twopence of your money, and I'll get the meal you want.'

" ' O thank you, Roswald!' said Sue;—' that will be such a help,—' and she ran for the pennies. and gave them into his hand.

" ' I'll be back presently,' said he; ' and then I'll tell you about things. Run up now after Mrs. Lucy.'

" ' I don't believe I need,' said Sue; ' they don't want anything of me.'

" ' Run up, though,' said Roswald; ' maybe

Mrs. Lucy will ask your mother too many questions.'

, " ' Why, that won't hurt her,' said Sue, laughing; but Roswald seemed in earnest, and she went up.

"Immediately Roswald set himself to build a fire. He knew where to go for wood, and he knew how to manage it; he soon had the hearth in order and a fine fire made ready; and it was done without a soil on his nice clothes and white linen. He was gone before Mrs. Lucy and Sue came down, but the snapping and sparkling in the chimney told tales of him.

" ' Why, he has made the fire for me!' cried Sue, with a very pleased face.

" ' Who made it?' said the lady

" ' Roswald.'

" ' That boy that was here when I came?'

" ' Yes, ma'am; he has made it for me.'

" ' Who is he?'

" ' He is Roswald Halifax.'

" ' What, the son of the widow, Mrs. Halifax?

" ' Yes, ma'am '

" ' And how came you to know him so well?'

" ' Why, I have always known him,' said Sue; ' that is, almost always. I used to know him a

great many years ago, when I went to school;
and he always used to take care of me, and give
me rides on his sleigh, and go on the beach with
me; and he always comes here '

'Is he a good boy?'

' 'Yes, ma'am; he's the best boy in the whole
place,' Sue said, with kindling eyes.

" 'I hope he is,' said Mrs. Lucy, ' for he has
nobody to manage him but his mother. I fancy
he has pretty much his own way.'

" 'It's a good way,' said Sue, decidedly. ' He
is good, Mrs. Lucy.'

" 'Does your mother want anything in particular, Sue?'

" Sue hesitated, and looked a little troubled.

" 'Tell me, dear; now, while your father is
away, you have no one to manage for you. Let
me know what I can do.'

" 'O Roswald would manage for us,' said Sue;
—' but——'

" 'But what?'

" The lady's manner and tone were very kind.
Sue looked up.

" 'She has nothing to eat, ma'am.'

" 'Nothing to eat!'

" 'No, ma'am; and I've only two shillings and

sixpence,—two shillings and fourpence, I mean,—
to get anything with; and I don't know what to
get. She can't eat what we can.'

" ' Have you nothing more to depend on but
that, my child?'

" ' That's all the money we have, ma'am.'

" ' And what have you in the house besides?
tell me, dear. We are all only stewards of what
God gives us; and what you want, perhaps, I can
supply.'

" Sue hesitated again.

" ' We haven't anything, Mrs. Lucy, but a
little Indian meal. Roswald is going to buy me
some more.'

" ' Are your father's affairs in so bad a condition, my child?'

" ' He can't get work, ma'am; if he could,
there would be no trouble. And what he does
he can't always get paid for.'

" ' And how long has this been the case, dear?'

" ' A long time,' said Sue, her tears starting
again,—' ever since a good while before mother
fell sick;—a good while before;—and then that
made it worse.'

" Mrs. Lucy looked at Sue a minute, and then
stooped forward and kissed the little meek fore-

head that was raised to her; and without another word quitted the house.

" Sue, with a very much brightened face, set about getting her porridge ready; evidently en joying the fire that had been made for her. She set on her skillet, and stirred in her meal; and when it was bubbling up properly, Sue turned her back to the fire and stood looking and medi-tating about something. Presently away she went, as if she had made up her mind. There was soon a great scraping and shuffling in the back room, and then in came Sue, pulling after her with much ado a big empty wooden chest, big enough to give her some trouble. With an air of business she dragged it into the middle of the room, where it was established solid and square, after the fashion of a table. Sue next dusted it carefully, and after it the counter and chairs, and mantel-shelf; the floor was clean swept always; and Sue herself, though in a faded calico, was as nice in her ways as her friend Roswald. Never was her little brown head any-thing but smooth-brushed; her frock clean; her hands and face as fair and pure as Nature had meant them to be. Roswald looked as if soil could not stick to him.

"When the room was in due state of nicety, Sue brought out and placed the two plates, the salt-cellar, with a little wooden spoon in it, the tumblers of blown glass, a pitcher of water, and the spoons. She had done then all she could, and she 'turned to watch her porridge and the front door both at once; for she did not forget to keep the porridge from burning, while her eye was upon the big brown door at every other minute.

"The porridge had been ready some time before the door at last opened, and in came Roswald bearing a large market-basket on his arm.

" 'It is astonishing,' said he, as he set it down, ' what a heavy thing Indian meal is ! '

" 'Why Roswald!' said Sue ;—' did you get all that with two cents ? '

" 'No,' said Roswald; ' the basket I borrowed. It is my mother's.'

" 'But have you got it full ? ' said Sue.

" 'Pretty full,' said Roswald, complacently.

" 'I never thought two cents would buy so much!' said Sue.

" 'Didn't you?' said Roswald. 'Ah, you're not much of a market-woman yet, Sue. My arm is tired.'

" 'I'm sorry!' said Sue.   'But I am so glad you have got it for me.'

" 'So am I.   Now is that porridge ready?'

" 'Ready this great while,' said the little house-keeper, carefully dishing it out.   'It's been only waiting for you.'

Roswald looked at her with a curious, gentle, sorrowful expression, which was as becoming as it was rare in a boy of his years.

" 'Are you hungry, Sue?'

" 'Yes,' said Sue, looking up from her dish with a face that spoke her perfectly satisfied with the dinner and the company.   'Aren't you?'

'Why, I ought to be. The air is sharp enough to give one an appetite.   Sue——'

" 'What?'

" 'Do you eat your porridge alone?'

" 'Not to-day,' said Sue, smiling, while an arch look came across her gentle eye.

" 'Does that mean that you are going to eat me with it?   I shall beg leave to interpose a stay of proceedings upon that.'

" And sitting down, with an air of determination, he drew the porridge dish quite to his end of the chest-table, and looked at Sue as much as to say, 'You don't touch it.'

· ·'What does that mean? Aren't you going to let me have any?' said Sue, laughing.

" ' No.'

" ' Why not?'

" ' I shall want all the porridge myself. You'll have to take something else, Sue!'

" ' But I haven't got anything else,' said Sue, looking puzzled and amused.

" ' Well, if you give me my dinner, it's fair I should give you yours,' said Roswald; and rising, he brought his market-basket to the side of the table, and sat down again.

" ' It's a pity I can't serve things in their right order,' he said, as he pulled out a quantity of apples from one end of the basket,—'but you see the dinner has gone in here head foremost. I never saw anything so troublesome to pack. There's a loaf of bread, now, that has no business to show itself so forward in the world; but here it comes —— Sue, you'll want a knife and fork.'

" And he set a deep, longish dish, with a cover, on the table, and then a flat round dish with a cover. Sue looked stupefied. Roswald glanced at her.

" ' Your appetite hasn't gone, Sue, has it?'

" But she got up and came round to him.

and put her face in her two hands down on his shoulder, and cried very hard indeed.

" ' Why, Sue ! ' said Roswald, gently,—' I never expected to see you cry for your dinner.'

" But Sue's tears didn't stop.

" ' I'll put all the things back in the basket if you say so,' said Roswald, smiling.

" ' I don't say any such thing,' said Sue, lifting up her tearful face and kissing his cheek ; and then she went round to her seat and sat down with her head in her hands. Roswald, in his turn, got up and went to her, and took hold of her hands.

" ' Come, Sue,—what's the matter ? that isn't fair. Look here, my porridge is growing cold.'

" And Sue laughed and cried together.

" ' Dear Roswald ! what made you do so ? '

" ' Do how ? '

" ' Why,—do *so*. You should n't. It was too good of you.'

" Roswald gave a merry little bit of a laugh, and began to take off the covers and put them on the counter

" ' Come, Sue,—look up ; I want my porridge, and I am waiting for you. Where shall I get a knife and fork ?- in the pantry in the back room ?

" Sue jumped up, wiping away her tears, and ran for the knife and fork; and from that time, throughout the rest of the meal, her face was a constant region of smiles.

" ' A roast chicken!—Oh, Roswald!—How mother will like a piece of that! How good it smells!'

" ' She's had her dinner,' said Roswald, who was carving : ' you must take a piece of it first. I ought in conscience to have had a separate dish for the potatoes, but my market-basket was resolved not to take it.   Some salt, Sue?'

" Sue ran for another knife and fork, and then began upon her piece of chicken; and Roswald helped himself out of his dish and eat, glancing over now and then at her.

" ' You can't think how good it is, Roswald, after eating porridge so long,' said Sue, with a perfectly new colour of pleasure in her face.

" ' This is capital porridge!' said Roswald. ' I'll trouble you for a piece of bread, Sue.'

" ' Why, Roswald!—are you eating nothing but porridge?'

" ' Yes, and I tell you I should like a piece of bread with it.'

" ' Ah, do take something else!' said Sue,

M

giving him the bread. ' The porridge will keep till another time.'

" ' I don't mean it shall, much of it,' said Roswald. ' It's the best dinner I've had in a great while.'

" Sue laid down her knife and fork to laugh at him, though the doing so had very near made her cry again.

" ' Please take some chicken, Roswald ! '

" ' I'd rather not. I'll take a piece of pie with you presently.'

" ' I should think chicken was enough,' said Sue ; ' you needn't have brought me pie.'

" ' I wanted some. It's a mince pie, Sue. Do you remember that day after to-morrow is Christmas ? '

" ' Christmas !—the day after to-morrow ! '— said Sue. ' No, I had forgot all about Christmas.'

" ' What shall we do to keep it ? '

" ' Why nothing, I sha'n't,' said Sue, meekly. ' I shall not eat porridge, Roswald. O if father could only come home—that would be enough keeping of Christmas ! We shouldn't want any thing else.'

" ' I'll tell you how it's going to be kept out of doors,' said Roswald ; ' it is fixing for a fine fall

of snow. The air is beginning to soften and
grow hazy already. I like a snowy Christmas.'

" ' With snow on the ground; but not snowing?'
said Sue

" ' Yes, both ways. Now, Sue,—have you another plate? or will you take it in your fingers?'

" Sue ran off for plates.

" ' How I wish I could give some of this to
father!' she said, as she tasted her first bit of
the pie. ' How will he get anything to eat, Roswald?'

" ' They will take care of that,' said Roswald.
' He will have a good dinner, Sue; you needn't
be concerned about it. If they didn't feed
their jurymen, you know, they might have no
jury by the time the cause was got through, and
that would be inconvenient Hasn't he been
home at all?'

" ' No.'

" ' They do sometimes let them come home,'
said Roswald; ' but in this case I suppose they
are keeping everybody tight to the mark '

" ' Why shouldn't they let them come home at
night?' said Sue; ' what would be the harm?
They must sleep somewhere '

" ' They are afraid, Sue, that if they let them

out of sight, somebody may talk to them about the cause, and put wrong notions into their heads; so that they won't give a true verdict.'

" ' What is a verdict?' said Sue.

" ' It's the jury's decision. You see, Sue, all the people—all the lawyers, on both sides,—will bring all the proof they can to show whether Simon Ruffin did or didn't shoot Mr. Bonny-castle. One side will try to prove he did, and the other side will try to prove he didn't. The jury will hear all that is to be said, and then they will make up their minds what is the truth. When they are ready, the judge will ask them, ' Gentlemen, are you agreed upon a verdict?' and the foreman will say, ' Yes.' Then the judge will ask, ' Is the prisoner at the bar guilty, or not guilty?' and the foreman will say, according as they have decided, ' Guilty,' or ' Not guilty;' and that answer is the *verdict.*'

" ' And then he will be hung! ' said Sue.

" ' If they find he is guilty, he will ; but they don't condemn him ; that's the judge's business. The jury only decide what is the truth.'

" ' Why must they have so many men to do that? why wouldn't one do as well?'

" ' It would, if they could be always sure of having a man who couldn't and wouldn't make a mistake. It isn't likely that twelve men will all make the same mistake.'

" ' And must they all be agreed ? ' said Sue

" ' They must all be agreed.'

" ' And if they are not, the man can't be hanged ? '

" ' No, nor set free.'

" ' I'm glad of that,' said Sue.

" ' Why, Sue ? '

" ' Because, if father isn't sure that man is guilty,—I mean, that he shot Mr. Bonnycastle,— he won't let them do anything to him.'

" ' It's well you can't be a juryman, Sue; you would never let any rogue have his rights.'

" ' Yes, I would,' said Sue, gravely; ' if I thought he deserved them.'

" ' I wouldn't trust you,' said Roswald. ' I should like to have you on the jury if I was standing a trial for my life. You'd be challenged. though.'

" ' Challenged ! ' said Sue

" ' Yes '

" ' What is that ? '

" ' Why, Simon Ruffin, for instance, might say, ' Mr. Peg is an old enemy of mine—he has a spite against me ; he would not be a fair judge in my case.' That would be challenging your father as an improper juryman, and he would be put out of the jury '

" ' But father isn't anybody's enemy,' said Sue.

" ' No, I know he isn't,' said Roswald, smiling; 'but that's an instance. Will you have some more pie, Sue ? '

" ' No, thank you. I'll put these things away, and see if mother wants anything; and then, if she don't, I'll come down, and we'll talk.'

" While Sue cleared away the dishes, Roswald mended the fire.

" ' You may as well let the table stand, Sue,' said he ; ' we shall want it again.'

" ' Why, are you coming to eat with me again ?' said Sue, laughing.

" ' I dare say I shall, if your father don't come home,' said Roswald.

" Sue soon came down-stairs, for her mother luckily did not want her ; and the two drew their chairs together and had a very long conversation, in the course of which Roswald gave many details of his stay at Merrytown, and enlightened Sue as to the charms and beauties of a country village. Sue looked and listened, and questioned and laughed; till there came a knocking up-stairs, and then they separated. Sue went up to her mother again, and Roswald left the house.

"The room did not look desolate any more, though it was left again without anybody in it. There was the chest-table, and the contented-looking fire, and the two chairs. All this while we shoes lay in the corner, and nobody looked at us. It seemed as if we were never to get done.

"The fire had died, the afternoon had not quite, when Mrs. Lucy came again. Her knock brought Sue down. She had come to bring another little pail of soup, and a basket with some bread and tea and sugar.

"'Don't spend your money, my child,' she said; 'keep it till you want it more. This will last your mother to-morrow, and I will see that you have something stronger than porridge.'

"'O I have, Mrs. Lucy,' said Sue, with a grateful little face, which thanked the lady better than words; 'I've got plenty for I don't know how long.'

"'You don't look as if you were out of heart,' said Mrs. Lucy. 'You know who can send better times?'

"'O yes, ma'am,' said Sue. 'He has already.'

"'Trust him, dear; and let me know all you want.'

"Sue stood, sober and silent, while Mrs.

Lucy went out at the door; and then she fell down on her knees before one of the chairs, and sunk her head on her hands; and was quite still for a minute or two, till the knocking sounded again. It was not a gentle tap on the floor, just to let Sue know she was wanted; it was an impatient, quarrelsome, vexatious, ' rat-tat-tat-tat-tat-tat!' 'rat-*tat*!' 'rat-*tat*!' Sue ran up.

" The cobbler did not come home that night, and Roswald would stay in the house. Sue did all she could to hinder him; for indeed there was nothing for him to sleep on but the pile of leather scraps; but he would not be hindered.

"'But your mother, Roswald?' Sue gently urged.

"'What of my mother?'

"'She will want you.'

"'How do you know that?'

"'I should think she would,' said Sue.

"'Should you? Well, she thinks, and so do I, that you want me more.'

"'How good you are, dear Roswald!'

"'Not very, Sue,' said Roswald, calmly.

"'Do you know what Mrs. Lucy says?' said Sue. 'She says that you have your own way in everything.'

"'Mrs. Lucy might have gone wider of the

mark, I suppose,' said Roswald, blowing up the fire.

"'Mrs. Lucy is very good,' said Sue. 'She brought us some tea and sugar this afternoon.'

"'Did she?' said Roswald. 'Then what will you do with what Mrs. Halifax sent?'

"'Did *she* send us some?' said Sue. 'Oh, Roswald!'

"Roswald laughed at her; and Sue did not know what to do with herself; she went and fetched down a quantity of coverlids and things for Roswald to wrap himself in, and be warm during the night; and begged him to keep a good fire.

"The next day still the cobbler did not come home. It passed with no visiters except Roswald and Mrs. Lucy, who stepped in for a minute. Sue's mother wanted her up-stairs pretty much the whole day; so there could be little fun going. Christmas-eve Roswald stayed in the house again. But he went off very early in the morning, without seeing Sue, after he had made the fire for her.

"The snow had not come so soon as Roswald thought it would. There was none on the ground Christmas-eve. But when Christmas-morning rose, the whole of Beachhead was softly and smoothly

covered with white. It had fallen very fast and
quietly during the night; the window-sills were
piled up, the door-knob was six inches high, and
the snow hung like thatch over the eaves of the
houses. The streets were a soft, pure, printless
spread of white.

"So they were early, when Roswald first went
out. And whatever kept people's feet within
doors — whether the dark morning, for the snow
still fell, or happy Christmas delays—there was
yet hardly a foot-print but his to be seen in that
part of the street when, some hours later, a sled
drawn by a horse and carrying two men and a
barrel, drew up before Mr. Peg's door. Sue had
heard the tinkle of the three bells which the
horse bore on his neck; and, as it told of the
first sleighing that year, she went to the window
to see. There was the sled and one man and
the barrel; the other man had jumped off, and
was knocking at the front door.

"'Very queer!' thought Sue;—'what can
they want here?'—but she ran down-stairs and
opened the door. The barrel was rolling up over
the snow to the house, and the two men were
behind pushing it. The cold air, and the yet
falling snow, and the white street, the men, and
the barrel rolling up towards Sue! Sue was

bewildered. But that barrel must go somewhere, and she held the door open.

"'What is it?' said Sue. 'It doesn't belong here, does it?'

"'There's 'Mr. Peg' on it,' said one of the men; 'and this is Mr. Peg's house, ain't it?'

"'What is it?' said Sue, in astonishment, as the barrel now stood up on end at the end of her chest-table.

"'It's a barrel of flour, I guess,' said the man. 'Looks like it; and it come from Mr. Hoonuman's.'

"'Flour!' said Sue.

"But the men with their heavy snow shoes clumped out again, and shut the door behind them with a bang Sue stood and looked.

"There was the barrel, full-sized, standing on end, one side of it still lightly coated with snow; and there were the snow-marks on the floor of the feet that had been there. It wasn't a dream. It was a real barrel, and even the snow wasn't in a hurry to melt away.

"Suddenly it flashed into Sue's little mind that it might be a Christmas!—and then whoever sent it ought to have been there, when the unwonted rosy colour sprang to her cheeks and made her for a minute look like a well-to-do child

And whoever sent it ought to have seen, a minute after, the bended head, and heard the thanksgiving that was not spoken, and the prayer, earnest and deep, for a blessing on the friend that had sent it.

" Sue had lifted her head, but had not moved from a foothold, when Roswald opened the door.

" ' O Roswald! do you see this ? '

" ' Merry Christmas, Sue ! ' said Roswald, gaily

" ' O Roswald, do you know what this is ? "

" ' It is very like a barrel of flour,' said Roswald. ' I should be surprised if it was anything else ! '

" ' But, Roswald, who sent it ? '

" ' Why, Sue !—Santa Claus, to be sure. Don't you know what day it is ? '

" ' It didn't come down chimney,' said Sue ; ' *that* I know. Dear Roswald, don't you know who sent it ? '

" ' If Santa Claus had taken me into his confidence, you know, Sue, it would not be an honest thing to betray. I wonder what you can do with a barrel of flour, now you have got it.'

" ' Do ? ' said Sue ;—but just then there was another knock at the door. Roswald opened it. In came a boy with a long string of fine black

and blue fish, which Mrs. Binch had sent to
Sue.

" ' Beachhead is waking up,' said Roswald.

" ' O Roswald ! ' said Sue, beginning to get
into the spirit of the thing,—' did you ever see
anything like those fish ? O tell Mrs. Binch
I thank her a great many times, please, —a great
many times ; I am *very* much obliged to her, and
so is father.—O Roswald !—do see !—'

" ' There's your mother knocking, Sue,' said
Roswald. ' Run off, and I'll take care of these
fish. You get ready for breakfast.'

" Sue went off in one direction, and Roswald
in another. He was the first to come back, with
a beautifully cleaned fish, which he soon had upon
the coals. He went on to set the table, and get
the bread and the tea ; and by that time Sue
came, as happy and as humble as possible, to
enjoy her breakfast. Whether or not Roswald had
had another breakfast before, he at any rate kept
her company in hers, both talking and eating.
The fish was declared to be the finest that could
come out of the sea, and Roswald was probably
adjudged to be the best cook on land ; if he had
been, his work could not have given better satisfaction

" Roswald had to go away after breakfast, and

told Sue his mother would want him at dinner, and he could not be there again before evening; but then he would come. Sue was satisfied with everything.

" Her day was spent for the most part up stairs But there were some breaks to it. A servant came in the course of the morning, bringing some bottles of wine for her mother, from Mrs. Halifax. Sue was already in a state of happiness that could hardly be heightened, and was in fact endeavouring to bear it with the help of her Bible, for it was in her hand whenever she came down stairs. But her eyes sparkled afresh at this gift, because it came from Mrs. Halifax, and because it was what her mother wanted. Sue could not wait. She begged the man to open one of the bottles for her; which with no little difficulty was done, without a corkscrew; and then, when he had gone, Sue poured out a little into a teacup, and went up stairs with such a face—joy and love were dancing a waltz in it.

" A little before noon there came another knock at the door. A modest knock this was, so gentle that Sue probably did not hear it. The knocker had not patience, or was not scrupulous; he opened the door halfway, and pushed in a square wooden box, nailed up and directed; after which he went away again, leaving it to tell its own tale.

"It seemed to tell nothing that Sue could understand. She looked at it, when next she came down, with all her eyes, and on all sides; but it was fast nailed up; she could not by any means open it, and she could not tell what was inside. She easily guessed that it was another 'Christmas;' but in what form? She sat and looked at it, with a face of infinite delight. She walked round it. Nothing was to be made of it but a pine-box, tolerably heavy, with her own name and her father's in large black letters on the upper side. Those letters did look lovely. Sue read them a great many times that day, and sat and gazed at the wooden box; but she could do nothing with it till Roswald came. He came at last, towards the edge of the evening. Sue was watching for him.

"'O Roswald, there you are!—here's another!'

"'Another what?' said Roswald, gravely.

"'Another Christmas—look here.'

"'Looks very like Christmas,' said Roswald.

"'Dear Roswald, won't you get a hammer!'

"'A hammer,' said Roswald. 'I suppose Mr Joist will lend me one'

" He went to borrow it, and opened the box. Sue watched with breathless interest while the hammer did its work, and the pieces of the cover came up one by one.

" ' Now, Sue!'—said Roswald, as he stepped back and began to draw the nails out of the wood.

" Sue drew the things out of the box with slow and cautious fingers, that seemed almost afraid of what they found. She did not say a word, but one or two half-breathed ' oh's! ' There was a nice and complete outfit of clothes for her. On the top lay a paper written with,

" ' *For little Susan Peg, from some friends that love her.*'

" When she got to the bottom, Sue looked up

" ' Oh, Roswald ! '

" ' Who sent me these ? '

" ' Some friends of little Susan Peg, that love her,' said Roswald.

" ' Did you know about it ? '

" ' I heard my mother speak about it, Sue.'

" ' Did *she* do it ? '

" ' Not she alone.   Mrs. Lucy and some other ladies all had a hand in it.'

" ' O how good they are !—'

" It was long before Sue could get up from the

box. Roswald stood, hammer in hand, looking at her and smiling. At last Sue packed the box again.

" ' I don't deserve it all,' she said ; ' but then I don't deserve anything. Now I guess we'll have some tea.'

" ' I'll go and carry back this hammer,' said Roswald, ' and then I'm ready. I'm very thirsty.'

" ' O dear Roswald !' said Sue, ' won't you, just open that barrel of flour first?—it will save going for the hammer again; and mother thinks she wants some pop-robin.'

" ' But what's pop-robin good for without milk?' said Roswald, as they went to the barrel, which he had rolled into the pantry.

" ' O now I might get a halfpenny's worth of milk,' said Sue ;—' it's for mother ; and now we have so many things, we might afford it.'

' ' See you don't,' said Roswald. ' Mother sends you word—there are enough nails in this barrel-head!—she says you may have as much milk as you want from her cow, whenever you will come for it or I will bring it; so between us I guess it'll be safe to count upon it.'

" He was hammering at the barrel-head, and Sue standing by looking very pleased, her little

N

hand gratefully resting on his shoulder, when another hand was laid on hers. Sue turned.

" ' Father!' she exclaimed. ' O father!—are you home?—O I'm so glad!—'

" The cobbler's grey head was stooped almost to the barrel-top, and Sue's arms were round his neck; and how many times they kissed each other I don't believe either of them knew. It seemed impossible for Sue to loose her hold.

" ' And *you* are here, my boy,' said the cobbler, turning to Roswald,—' doing my work!'

" ' No, sir, I have been doing *mine,*' said Roswald.

" ' O father, he has taken such care of me!' said Sue.

" ' I warrant him,' said the cobbler. ' If I could only have known that Roswald Halifax was in town, I could have minded my business with some quietness.'

" ' And is it done, father?' said Sue

" ' It is done, my child.'

" ' And what have you done with that man?'

" ' We have declared him upon our judgment, *Not Guilty.'*

" ' O I'm so glad!' said Sue.

" They came back to their tea, all three; and more black fish was broiled; and all the Christ-

mas was told over; and well-nigh all the trial.
The jury had been kept in all Christmas-day to
agree upon their verdict.

"From that day the cobbler's affairs improved.
Whether his friends exerted themselves to better
his condition, now that they knew it; or whether
Mr. Ruffin's friends did; or whether neither did,
but other causes came into work, certain it is
that from that time the cobbler's hands had
something to do; and more and more till they had
plenty. So it came to pass that this poor pair
of shoes didn't get finished till about a month
ago; and then Mr. Krinken must take it into
his head that we would fit his little boy, and
bought us;—for which we owe him a grudge, as
we wanted decidedly to spend our lives with Mr.
Peg and his little brown-headed daughter."

"Did Mrs. Peg get well?" said Carl.

"Yes, long ago, and came down-stairs; but she
was no improvement to her family, though her
getting well was."

"I am very sorry that story is done," said
Carl. "I want to hear some more about Roswald
Halifax."

"There is no more to tell," said the shoe.

If Carl had been puzzled on Friday as to what story he would hear, he was yet more doubtful on Saturday. There lay the pine-cone, the hymn-book, and the stocking, on the old chest, and there sat Carl on the floor beside them,—sometimes pulling his fingers, and sometimes turning over the three remaining story-tellers, by way of helping him to make up his mind. As a last resort he was taking a meditative survey of the ends of his toes, when a little shrill voice from the chest startled him; and the pine-cone began without more ado

THE STORY OF THE PINE CONE.

" ' Whew!' said the north wind   ' Whew—r—r—r—r!

" The fir trees heard him coming, and bowed their tall heads very gracefully, as if to tell the wind he could not do much with them.   Only some of the little cones who had never blown about a great deal, felt frightened, and said the wind made their teeth chatter.

" ' Do you think we can stay on?' asked one little cone ; and the others would have said they didn't know, but the wind gave the tree such another shake that their words were lost.

" ' Whew—r—r—r—r—r!' said the wind.

" And again the fir trees bowed to let him pass, and swayed from side to side, and the great branches creaked and moaned and flung themselves about in a desperate kind of way ; but the leaves played sweet music.   It was their fashion whenever the wind blew

" ' I think we shall have snow,' said the tallest of the fir trees, looking over the heads of his com panions.

" ' The sky is very clear,' remarked a very small and inexperienced fir, who was so short he could not see much of anything.

" ' Yes,' said the tall one, ' so you think; but there is a great deal of sky besides that which is over our heads; and I can see the wind gathering handfuls of snow-clouds, which he will fling about us presently.'

" ' Yes,'—repeated the tall fir, with another graceful bend—' I see them—they are coming.'

" The evergreens were all sorry to hear this, for nothing depressed them so much as snow; the rain they could generally shake off,—at least if it didn't freeze too hard.

" As for the beeches, they said if that was the case they must put off their summer clothes directly. And one little beech, with a great effort, did succeed in shaking off half-a-dozen green leaves the next time the wind came that way.

" ' You need not hurry yourselves,' said the tall fir—' this is only an early storm—the winter will not come yet. I can still see the sun for a few minutes every day.'

" And that was true. For a few minutes the sun shewed himself above the horizon, and then after making a very small arch in the sky, down he went again. Then came the long afternoon of clear twilight ; and the longer night, when the stars threw soft shadows like a young moon, and looked down to see their bright eyes in the deep fiord that lay at the foot of the fir trees. For this was on the north-west side of Norway ; and the fir trees grew by one of the many inlets of the sea which run far away for miles into the country, and are called fiords.

" At the mouth the fiord was so narrow, and the overhanging trees so thick, that you might have coasted along, backwards and forwards, without perceiving the entrance ; but to the country people it was well known, and unmistakeably marked out by one particular hemlock. Pushing your little boat through its green branches that dipped their fingers in the water, the fiord opened before you. The banks on each side were for the most part very steep, and often wooded to the water's edge ; while sometimes a pitch of bare rocks and a noisy cataract came rough and tumble down together, pouring disturbance into the smooth waters of the fiord.

" The fiord itself was too beautiful to be half

described. It wound about from rock to rock,
now swashing gently at the base of a high mountain, and then turning and spreading out, bay-
like, where the shore was lower and the hills stood
aloof; but everywhere overhung or nodded to
by the great trees that looked as if they had
known it since it was a mere rill,—the beeches
and oaks and hemlocks, the tall pines like a
ship's mainmast; and most of all by that glory
of those forests—the Norway Spruce fir. These
watched the fiord everywhere,—in the regions of
perfect solitude, and in the spots where a little
clearing—a waft of blue smoke—the plaintive bleat
of a goat mounting up in the world, or the hearty
bow-wow of some hardy little dog, that was
minding his own business and everybody's else,
told of a human habitation. Back of all—beyond
cliff and wood and everything but the blue sky,
towered up the peaks of perpetual snow—whose
bare heads no man had ever seen.

" The fiord could not point heavenward after that
fashion. But it reflected every bit of blue that
came over it, and even when the skies were dark,
and the snow-peaks hid their heads in a cloud,
the fiord's reflections were only grave and thoughtful—never gloomy.

" And the water was so clear !

" Sailing along in a little boat you could look down, down, for twenty fathoms, and see the smooth white sand, with little shells and star-fish; and then the bottom of the fiord rose suddenly up like a rocky mountain—over which the boat passed into a deep gulf on the other side. Then came a plain, and great forests, far down in the water; through which large fishes swam softly about; and then another mountain.

" In one of the narrowest parts of the fiord a little spot of cleared and cultivated land lay like a smile between it and the rough mountain. A mere point of land—a little valley wedged in among the heights that rose cliff beyond cliff towards the blue sky, fringed here and there with fir trees. The valley smiled none the less for all this roughness; and the little dwelling that there found a foothold seemed rather to court the protection of the cliffs, and to nestle under their shelter. The house was such as best suited the place.

" It was built of great pine logs, roughly squared and laid one upon another, with layers of moss between; while every crevice and crack was well stuffed with the same. The roof was of boards, covered with strips of birch bark; and over all a coating of earth two or three inches deep in

which a fine crop of moss had taken root. The
windows were large, and well glazed with coarse
glass, while very white curtains hung within; and
the door was painted in gay colours. Other little
huts or houses stood about, forming a sort of
square; and furnishing apartments for the pig,
the cows, and their winter provision; while one
more carefully built than the rest, held all manner of stores for the family. Raised upon posts,
that the rats might not enter, the little alpebod
kept safe the fish, the venison, the vegetables,—
even the cloth, yarn, and sometimes clothing, of
its humble owners.

" In sight of the house, a little way down the
fiord, was a wild ravine; skirted on one side with
a height of thick woods and rocks, while on the
other the rocks stood alone—the sharp ridge rising
up hundreds of feet to a ledge in some places not
a foot wide. On either side the ridge the pitch
was very sheer down, the one depth being filled
with forest trees which led on to the wooded hill
beyond; while the ravine on the other echoed to
the voice of a waterfall, that pouring down over a
pile of rocks perhaps two hundred feet high,
foamed into the fiord; which then came eddying
past the little hut, bearing the white flakes yet
on its blue water

" This was all one could see in the valley; but the tall fir trees looked at long ranges of wooded hills and rocky cliffs, with the fiord in its further windings, and beyond all the snow mountains.

" ' How cold you must be up there!' said a little pine who was nearly as high as the tall fir's lower branches. But the fir did not hear him, or perhaps did not take notice, for he was looking off at the fine prospect

" ' Yes, it is cold up here,' answered one of the fir cones,—' and windy—and there's a great deal of sameness about it. It's just snow and rain, and wind and sunshine, and then snow again.'

" ' That's what it is everywhere,' said the wind as he swept by.

" ' I can't help it,'—said the cone—' I am tired of it. I want to travel, and see the world, and be of some use to society. What can one do in the top of a fir tree?'

" ' Why, what can a pine cone do anywhere?' said some of the beech mast.

" ' The end of a pine cone's existence is not to be eaten up, however,' retorted the cone, sharply. ' Neither am I a pine cone—though people will call me so. We firs hold our heads pretty high, I can tell you. But I will throw

myself into the fiord some day, and go to sea. I
have no doubt I could sail as well as a boat. It
would be fine thing to discover new islands, and
take possession.'

" ' It would be very lonely,' said a squirrel
who was gathering beech mast.

" ' Royally so—' said the pine cone. ' There
one would be king of all the trees.'

" ' The trees never had but one king, and that
was a bramble,' said a reed at the water's edge
who was well versed in history.

" ' What nonsense you are all talking!' said the
tall fir tree at length. ' My top leaf is at this
moment loaded with a snowflake—there is something sensible for you to think of.'

" At this moment the hut door opened and a
woman came out.

" She wore a dark stuff petticoat made very
short, with warm stockings and thick shoes ; a
yellow close-fitting bodice was girdled round her
waist, and from under it came out a white kerchief
and very full white sleeves. On her head she
wore a high white cap.

" She looked first at the weather, and then
turning towards the fall she watched or listened
for a few minutes,—but water and rocks and firs
were all that eye or ear could find out. Then

going up to a line stretched between two of the fir-trees, she felt of some things that hung there to dry."

" I s'pose that was her clothes line," said Carl.

" No it wasn't," replied the cone,—" I might rather call it her *bread* line. The things that hung there were great pieces of the inner bark of the pine tree, and looked very much like sheets of foolscap paper."

" She didn't make bread out of *them*, I guess," said Carl.

" Yes she did," replied the cone. " She made many a loaf of bark bread, by pounding the dry bark and mixing it with flour. It wasn't particularly bad bread either. So people say—I never tasted it. But the country folks in Norway use it a great deal in hard seasons; and in those woods you often meet great pine trees that have been stripped of their bark, and that have dried and bleached in the weather till they look as if made of bone or marble.

" Well—the pieces of bark were dry, and Norrska began to take them off the line, for of course the snow would not improve them."

" Who was Norrska?" interrupted Carl.

" The good woman that came out of the house.

She took them down, and when they were all in a heap at the foot of the tree she began to carry them off to the alpebod—that is the little store-house I spoke of. Then she went back into the hut for a minute, and when she came out again she had on a long-sleeved grey woollen jacket, and her luur in her hand."

" What's that?" said Carl.

" The luur is a long trumpet-shaped thing, made of hollow pieces of wood, or pieces of birch bark, tied together, and four or five feet long."

" What was it for?" said Carl.

" Why you shall hear, if you will have patience," said the cone. " Norrska raised the luur with one hand, and putting her mouth to the little end there came forth of the other sundry sweet and loud sounds, which echoed back and forth among the rocks till they died away, far up the mountain."

" But I say," said Carl, " what for?"

And he took hold of the pine cone and gave it a little pinch; but it was pretty sharp and he let go again.

The pine cone settled himself down on the chest, looking just as stiff as ever, and then went on with his story.

" Norrska sounded her luur twice or thrice,

and presently the head and horns of a red cow shewed themselves high up among the rocks. Then came in sight her shoulders and fore feet, and her hind feet and tail; and the whole cow began to descend into the valley, while a dun cow's head shewed itself in just the same place and fashion. But when Norrska had once seen that they were coming she ceased to watch them, and turned to the fall again.

" Its white foam looked whiter than ever in the gathering dusk. The grey clouds which were fast closing in overhead sent down a cold grey light, and the water before it broke no longer sparkled with the sun's gay beams, but looked leaden and cold and deep. Then breasted with snow like the stormy petrel, it came flying down the precipice, to plunge into the deep fiord below. Its very voice seem changed; for the wind had died away, and the steady roar of the water was the only sound that broke the hush.

" There was no living creature in sight,—unless a little lemming peeped out of his hole, or an eagle soared across the sky, a mere speck upon its clouds. The cows had reached the valley and now stood quietly chewing the cud, having had the precaution to turn their backs to the wind; and now Norrska fetched the milkpails, and drove

the red cow up to the milking-corner. And as
she went, a snowflake fell on her forehead and
another fell on top of her head; and the fir trees
sighed, and bowed their heads to what they
couldn't help. Norrska sighed too.

" ' The winter is coming,' she said, ' and the
snow; and truly the alpebod is but poorly filled.
And Sneeflocken sick—and Laaft not home from
Lofoden!—And Kline—what can keep him?'
And again she looked towards the fall.

" Kline was there now—she could see him
plain enough, though he was but a little spot on
that sharp ridge by the waterfall. The path
itself was hard to find, as it wound about over
and under and around the points of rock that
met on the ledge. A stranger could scarce have
climbed it but on hands and knees. Yet down
there came Kline, sure-footed as a chamois—
swiftly down; and singing praises of the rocks
and streams and woods and snow as he came.
But before he reached the foot of the hill Kline's
song stopped,—with the first look at the hut his
thoughts had outrun his feet; and with a quieter
step now he came down into the valley and up
to where his mother sat milking the red cow. In
one hand was a gun, in the other a string of
golden plovers.

" ' How late, Kline ! ' said Norrska.

" ' Yes mother—I tried to get shot at a rein-deer. How is she?'

" Norrska silently pointed to a snowflake, which falling on her hand as she talked, had lain for a moment in all its pure beauty, but was now melting fast away. She watched till it disappeared, and then bending her head lower than ever, she resumed her work.

" Kline stood silent and thoughtful.

" ' May be not, mother,' he said at length. ' Her appetite has been better lately. See—I have these plovers for her to-night, and to-morrow I will have the deer. Think of my finding one in these parts!'

" But his mother said no more, and when the pails were full Kline took them from her and carried them into one of the little huts; and then returning he drove the cows into their little log dwelling, and taking up his birds and gun he walked slowly to the house. But the gayly-painted door was out of tune with his mood, and he turned and went round the back way.

" Leaving both gun and birds in the kitchen, Kline opened softly a door leading to one of the bedrooms and went in.

" The corners of this room and the sides of

the windows were boarded, and the floor was strewed with fresh twigs of the juniper tree; which gave a sweet smell through the room, and made it look pretty too. Of the three windows two looked towards the fiord and one to the mountain and over the little clearing. The bed stood in a recess that had doors like one of your cupboards; but these now were open, and by the bedside stood a little white pine table, and upon it a wooden bowl and spoon—all prettily carved."

" How were they carved?" said Carl.

" The bowl had carved upon it a spray of the wild bramble—twining round with its leaves and berries; and the handle of the spoon was like a wild duck's head; and the feet of the table were like bear's feet. Kline had done it all, for in Norway the men and boys carve a great deal, and very beautifully; and this bowl and spoon had been made for his little sister as he sat by her bedside, and Kline was very proud of them. The feathers on the duck's head were beautifully done, and the bramble-berries looked pretty enough to eat. But Kline did not once look at them now, for something far prettier lay on the bed, and that was little Sneeflocken."

" What did they call her that for?" said Carl.

" Because that is the name of the snowflakes.
And she was just as pure and fresh as they, and
had never had the least bit of colour in her
cheeks from the time she was a baby. You could
scarcely have distinguished them from the pillow,
but for the fair hair that came between. She
was covered with a quilt made of down; for
Kline had risked his life almost in climbing to
the high difficult places where the eider ducks
build their nests, that he might get the soft down
which the mother duck plucks from her own
breast to keep her eggs and nestlings warm.
And Norrska had made it into a quilt, the warmest
thing that could be—while the weight of it was
almost nothing.

" And beneath this soft quilt Sneeflocken lay,
with her eyes closed, and singing softly to herself
in the Norse language a hymn, which was something like this :—

' O little child, lie still and sleep !—
    Jesus is near,
    Thou need'st not fear;—
No one need fear, whom God doth keep
    By day or night.
Then lay thee down in slumber deep
    Till morning light.

O little child, thou need'st not wake ;—
　　Though bears should prowl,
　　And wolfish howl
And watch-dog's bark the silence break.
　　Jesus is strong,—
And angels watch thee for his sake,
　　The whole night long.

O little child, lie still and rest,—
　　He sweetly sleeps
　　Whom Jesus keeps,—
And in the morning wake, so blest,
　　His child to be.
Love every one, but love him best,—
　　He first loved thee.

O little child ! when thou must die,
　　Fear nothing then,—
　　But say Amen
To God's command ; and quiet lie
　　In his kind hand,
Till he shall say, ' Dear child, come, fly
　　To heaven's bright land.'

Then with thy angel-wings quick grown,
　　Shalt thou ascend,
　　To meet thy Friend,—
Jesus the little child will own—
　　Safe, at his side !
And thou shalt live before the throne
　　Because he died !'

" Kline had to step back into the shadow of the door of the recess, to wipe the tears off his face, before he could venture to speak to his little sister. But she spoke first.

" ' Kline ! '

" ' What, dear?' said her brother, coming forward.

" ' I thought I heard your step,' said Sneeflocken with a smile, and putting up her lips to kiss him. ' Where have you been all day?'

" ' O — over the mountains — hunting,' said Kline as cheerfully as he could. ' I saw a great big reindeer, Flocken ; and I mean to go and find him to-morrow. That would fill the alpebod finely, and you would like some venison—wouldn't you dear ?'

" ' O yes,' said Flocken—with a little smile— ' but *I* wouldn't kill the deer for that.'

" ' I would,' said Kline. ' And it would help mother, too.'

" ' I should like to help mother, if I could,' said Sneeflocken, putting her little thin hands together. ' But Jesus will—I have asked him.'

" ' Why you help us all,' said Kline ; ' just as the birds do when they sing, or the sun when it shines.'

" 'Maybe I shall by and by,' said the child, smiling again in that grave, quiet way.

" ' Yes, by and by,—when you grow up to be a strong woman,' said Kline.

" 'No, Kline,' said Sneeflocken stroking his face—' No, dear Kline—but by and by when I go to heaven. Maybe God will let me help take care of her then, and of you too, Kline. But you will not know that it is your little Snee flocken.'

" And Kline could only sit and hold her in his arms, and say nothing.

" The snow fell all that night, and the winter set in early; and the waterfall scattered icicles upon every branch and rock in its way, and then built for itself an ice trough through which it poured down as noisily as ever. Then the sun never shewed his face but for a few minutes, and the rest of the day was twilight. And at night the moon shone splendidly, and the Northern Lights showed peaks of fire in the heavens,—or sometimes there were only the stars, burning clear in the high lift, and twinkling down in the dark fiord between the shadows of the fir trees. Now and then a bear would come out, and prowl about the little dwelling,—or a wolf gave a concert

with the waterfall; but cows and pigs were safe
shut up; and Foss, the little dog, shewed so
much disapprobation at the concert, that often the
wolves did not have one for nights together.
Laaft, the father of Kline, got home from
Lofoden with his stock of dried fish; and Kline
himself had shot his reindeer; and both meat
and fish were safely stowed in the alpebod.
Didn't the wolves know that! and didn't their
mouths water sometimes at night till they
were fringed with icicles! But they never tried
to break in, for the alpebod was strong; and
little Foss knew as well as the wolves what
good things were there; and scolded terribly if
every body and every thing did not keep at a
respectful distance. And besides all that, the
wolves were afraid of the light that always shone
from one room of the little cottage.

" 'This is a very quiet way of life—ours,' said
the fir trees nodding to each other.

" ' I'm very tired of it,' said one of the cones.
' It's very cold up here, and really in the dark
one cannot see to do much.'

" ' A fir glories in the frost and the cold and
the snow,' said the tall tree proudly. ' We are
not called upon to do anything but to make sweet
music to the wind, and to keep it from blowing

too fiercely upon the little hut, and to shew our fine heads against the sky. The snow-birds are warm in our arms during the long night, for *we* have plenty of good clothes all the year round.'

" The beeches heard this speech, but were too frost-bound to make any answer."

" What became of the discontented pine cone?" said Carl. "Did he throw himself into the fiord?"

" Yes," said the cone,—" at least one night he tried to. But he fell on the shore instead—just dropped down at the foot of the fir tree; and there Kline found him one day, and picked him up and carried him into the house to show Flocken—he was such a large one.

" Every night through the winter was that light burning in the same room of the hut; and every day did Kline come out with his gun and spend what daylight there was in hunting. Sometimes he brought home a hare or a ptarmigan, or a partridge that he had snared, or a wild duck; while his father was cutting wood, or away in his boat to catch fish.

" ' I could get only one partridge to-day, dear Flocken,' Kline would say upon his return home; ' but maybe I shall find something better to-morrow.'

" ' O Kline,' said his little sister, ' how good

you are to take so much trouble for me! But
it's a pity to kill the birds,—they can't make me
live, so we might let them.'

" 'Wasn't that a good one you had yesterday?' said Kline.

" 'O yes—' said Flocken,—'it was delicious.
I think everything is good that you get for me
and that mother cooks. But then you know I
can't eat much.'

" If you had seen her as she lay there—so
thin, so white,—you might as soon have suspected
a very snowflake of eating much.

" 'So it don't make much difference,' repeated
little Sneeflocken, 'what I have; only I do believe, Kline, that I like to have you take so much
trouble, and go away up in the snow to get things
for me.' And she put her arms round his neck,
and laying her white face against his coarse grey
jacket, she stroked and caressed him until Kline
thought his heart would burst beneath the
weight of that little snowflake.

" 'When the spring comes,' he said, 'we will
go up the mountain and look for flowers; and I
will make you a wreath of violets and fringed
pinks, little Flocken.'

" Sneeflocken stroked his face and smiled, and
then she looked grave again

-" ' And forget-me-nots, Kline,' she said softly,—
' you will want them too. The little blue forget-
me-nots—they are so like the sky-colour. You
will think about me, Kline, whenever you see
them, for I shall know what the sky is made of
then.—Where's mother ?'

" ' She is cooking your partridge,' said Kline.
' Don't you smell it?'

" ' O yes,' said the child smiling, ' and I guess
the wolves smell it too. How loud they howl !'

" ' You are not afraid of them ?' said her
brother tenderly.

" ' No—' said Sneeflocken with a strange look
of weakness and trust upon her little face. ' No
—I am not afraid of them, for the Good Shepherd
is very strong. I should be, if it wasn't for
that. How kind he is, Kline, to think about
such poor little children as we are! And it's
kind of him to take me away, too, for I'm not
very strong—I don't think I could ever be of
much use.'

" ' You are of too much use, my little Sneeflocken,' said Kline, sadly, ' because we shouldn't
know what to do without you.'

" ' Why you will have me then,' said the child
looking up in his face. ' Just as you have the
flowers now, Kline. And you can think about

me, and say that some day you will go up and up
to find me.'

" 'Up to find you!' said Laaft, who with
Norrska had just entered the room. 'Are you
going to play hide-and-seek with Kline upon the
mountains, my little dear?'

" But Norrska asked no such questions, for
she knew what Sneeflocken meant well enough;
but she brought the roast partridge to the bedside, on a little wooden platter that had a row of
pine cones carved all round the edge; and sitting
down on the bed she watched the child eat her
scanty supper when Kline had lifted her up and
wrapped an old cloak about her.

" Little Foss had followed them in, and now
he sat wagging his tail and beating the floor with
it, just because he felt uncomfortable and didn't
know what to do with himself—not at all because
he smelt the partridge   For he knew perfectly
well that Sneeflocken was sick; and when she
had finished her supper, and called 'Foss! Foss!'
—the little dog ran to the bed, and, standing as
high as he could on his hind legs thrust his cold
nose into her hand, and whined and whimpered
with joy and sorrow. Then in a tumult of excitement, he dashed out of the house to bark at
the wolves again

" They watched her so, by day and by night, through the long winter; but before the first spring days came, the little snowflake had melted away and sunk down into the brown earth.

" They made her grave within the little clearing, just between the house windows and the mountain; where the fir tree shadows could just touch it sometimes, but where the sunlight came as well. And within the little white railing that enclosed the grave they placed an upright slab of wood, upon which Kline had carved these words as Norrska desired him :—

"' SAY UNTO HER,—IS IT WELL WITH THEE ? IS IT WELL WITH THY HUSBAND ? IS IT WELL WITH THE CHILD ? AND SHE ANSWERED, IT IS WELL.'

" The grass grew green and fresh there, and the little blue forget-me-nots that Kline had planted about the grave soon covered it with their flowers. And sometimes when Kline stood there leaning over the paling, he almost fancied that it was as she said,—that God had sent her to take care of them ; and that it was not the soft spring wind which stroked his face, but the hand of his little Sneeflocken.

" He thanked God that she was safe in the arms of the Good Shepherd, and for the hope that when his time came to go, he should find her in heaven."

" Were you that discontented pine cone?" said Carl, when he had sat for some time thinking over the story.

" Yes," said the cone, " and I was carried into the house as I told you. And then because Sneeflocken had once held me in her little hand, Kline said he would keep me always."

" But I say!" said Carl, knitting his brows and looking very eager; "how did you get *here?*"

" Because other people were as foolish as I was, and didn't know when they were well off." said the cone. " For Kline was your mother's grandfather; and when he died, and she left her home to follow the fortunes of John Krinken, she brought the old pine cone along; to remember the tall fir trees that waved above the old hut in Norway, and to remind her of little Foss, and Kline, and Sneeflocken."

THE STORY OF THE HYMN BOOK.

" ' Clary! Clary !—wake up! you'll be late
See how late it's getting.'

" ' Well mother—but I'm so tired! What's
the good of living so, mother?'

" ' One must live somehow, child—till one's
time comes to die.'

" Clary did not say, but she thought, as she
raised herself slowly from the hard little straw
bed, that it did not matter how soon that time
came for her. Work! work !—living to work
and working to live. Working hard, too, and
for what a pittance of life! Was it *living* to
sleep half as much as she wanted, and then to
get up in the cold grey dawn of a winter's
morning, get three or four dirty children out of
bed and into such clothes as they had ; and then
after as much breakfast as she had had sleep, to
take that long cold walk in her old straw bonnet

and thin cotton shawl to the printing-office,—there to stand all day supplying the busy iron fingers of the press? How thin and blue her own were!

" Poor Clary!—In truth she did not know what it was to *live*, in the real sense of the word—her mind looked back to no happier time than the present; for though she could well remember being a dirty little child like her brothers and sisters, with nothing to do but play or quarrel as she felt inclined, yet she by no means wished the time back again The death of her father, and the consequent absence of his bottle and his wild fits of intoxication, had left the family in a peaceful state compared with those days; and since Clary had been at the printing-office she had learned to love the sight of decently-dressed people—had begun to take more pains to look nice herself; and above all, had begun to feel that she would like to be happy and well-dressed and respectable, if she only knew how. But they were very, very poor, and there were a cluster of little mouths to fill,—as clamorous and wide open as a nest of young swallows,—and never saying 'enough.' So though she kept her face cleaner and her hair smoother, and, when she could get them sewed hooks and eyes on her dress,—the march of im

provement rested there; and her face was as hope-
less, her eye as dull, as ever. For nobody had ever
taught Clary about that ' one thing needful' which
can make up for the want of all others. She had
never been to church, she had never read the
Bible—and indeed had none to read. She thought
that nothing but money could make them happy,
—she thought nobody could want anything but
money; and was really not much surprised that
people were so loath to part with it. They must
be that, she thought, or the poor press-tenders
could not be so very far removed from the heads
of the concern, in comfortable appearance.

" There were many of the women indeed that
spent more upon their dress than she did. A
tawdry silk jacket worked all day at her right
hand, and a pair of earrings dangled all day before
her; while her own dress was but the coarsest
calico ; but Clary had somehow begun to wish for
neatness and comfort,—of course finery was forgotten.

." Never had she been much inclined to envy
anybody, till one day the head printer brought his
two little children to the office; and Clary's
heart beat quick time to her sorrowful thoughts
all the hours after. O to see those children at
home with clean faces, and smooth hair, and whole

frocks and trousers! And now there were rags and dirt and tangled locks, and no time to mend matters; and small stock of soap and combs and needles to mend with. Clary went straight to bed when she got home that night; and it was on the next morning that she awoke with the question,

" ' Mother, what's the use of living so?'

" But as her mother had said, she must live somehow; and getting wearily out of bed, hastily too, for it was indeed late, Clary easily found her way into such clothes as she had; and then, having with some difficulty fastened the children into theirs, she seated them at the table where her mother had by this time placed the breakfast; and herself stood by, drinking a cup of the miserable coffee and tying on her bonnet at the same time.

" ' Going to wash to-day, mother?'

" ' Yes.'

" ' Then I'll take some bread and not try to come home for dinner.'

" This was the ordinary course of things. Clary at the printing-press, and her mother doing days' work for people well off in the world; while the younger children were locked in or locked out, as the case might be.

p

" It was a foggy December morning,—not very cold, but with a drizzling mist that was more chilling than snow; and by the time Clary reached the office she felt as moody and uncomfortable as the weather. It was warm enough in the office, but not very cheering she thought; though some of the men looked as if they enjoyed life sufficiently well, as with sleeves rolled up they whistled softly over their work, keeping time with their heads if the tune were a particularly lively one.

" Clary put her bonnet and shawl in their place, and went to the press she always tended. It was motionless now, and a man was just putting in a new set of plates. Clary hardly noticed what he was doing—it mattered so little to her what words were printed on those great sheets of paper that she handled every day; though she could read, and very well; but stood listlessly.

" 'What's the matter, Clary?' said the man 'You look dumpish this morning. I've fixed you a new piece of work here that'll be good for that— they say poetry's firstrate for the spirits.'

" Something good for her! She knew the man spoke jestingly, and yet as he walked off Clary thought she would look and see what it was that he was talking about. She had seen type enough to be able to spell it out backwards, and bending over the plates she read at the corner next her,—

' O how happy'—

" And then the machine was suddenly put in motion; and not faster could she supply the sheets than the press drew them in, printed them, and tossed them out in a nice pile at one end.

" Clary could not stop for one instant. But she had something to think about. Again and again she repeated those three words to herself, and wondered of whom they spoke, and what could be the rest of the sentence. She could guess,—it must mean the people who were rich, and had plenty of clothes, and plenty to eat, and time to sleep and to walk about in the sunshine. The people who bought the meats that she saw hanging up in the butchers' shops, which she hardly knew by name and much less by taste,—the beautiful ladies that she sometimes saw in Broadway when she happened to get through work a little earlier than usual—wrapped up in furs and velvets and looking as if they wouldn't know calico when they saw it,—the children that she had seen looking out of carriage windows with little white lapdogs; the curling ears on the head of the dog and the curling feathers on the head of the child

seeming to Clary almost equally beautiful. Yes,
those must be the happy people; but then she
would very much like to know more about them—
to read all those stories which the press was no
doubt printing off, of these same happy people—
who never were poor and who had no little ragged
brothers and sisters. For the first time in her life
Clary wished the press would get out of order, for
some other reason than because she was tired. Her
mind worked and worked upon those three words
till she was almost wild with the desire to read
more. Perhaps it told the way to be rich and
happy,—and that cruel press kept moving just as
fast as it could. Not till twelve o'clock did it make
a pause. But at twelve o'clock there was a sudden
hush; and hardly had the rollers stopped their
rolling, before Clary had left her place and gone to
that corner of the pile of printed sheets where she
knew the words must be. Yes, they were there—
she found them easy enough; but what were they?

> ' O how happy are they
> *Who the Saviour obey,*
> *And have laid up their treasure above.'*

" Poor Clary! she could almost have cried over
her disappointment; for if the words had been
Greek she could hardly have been more puzzled

as to their meaning. As I have said, she had never been to church—she had never read the Bible;—and if ever she had heard the Saviour's name, it was from those who spoke it with neither love nor reverence. Her father had been a drunkard,—her mother was a hard-working, well-meaning woman, but as ignorant as Clary herself. No preacher of the gospel had ever set foot in their house,—and 'how should they believe on him of whom they had not heard?'

" So Clary puzzled over the lines and could make nothing of them. The word *treasure* she did indeed understand; but where it was to be laid up, and how, were as far from her as ever And constantly her mind went back to that second line—' *Who the Saviour obey.*'

" ' I wonder if I couldn't do that?' she thought to herself,—' if I only knew how. Mother always said I was good about minding. It must be so pleasant to be happy.—It doesn't say that nobody can do it but rich people, either,'—and again she read the words. They were at the bottom of the sheet, and the next might not come to her press at all, or not for some days. She looked over the rest of the sheet. A great many of the hymns she could make nothing of at all,—the very words —' missionary,' and ' convert,' and ' ransom,

were strange to her. Then this hymn caught her
eye, and she read,—

> " Come to the mercy-seat,—
> " Come to the place of prayer ; .
> " Come, little children, to his feet,
> " In whom ye live and are.

> " Come to your God in prayer—
> " Come to your Saviour now—
> " While youthful skies are bright and fair,
> " And health is on your brow."

" Clary read no further. That did not suit
her, she thought—there was nothing bright about
her way of life or herself. It seemed the old
thing again—the happy rich people. She went
back and read the first one over,—that did not
seem so, and she sought further; wearily glancing from hymn to hymn, but with a longing that
not even the hard words could check. At last
she saw one verse, the first word of which she
knew well enough,—

> " Poor, weak, and worthless, though I am,
> " I have a rich almighty Friend,—
> " Jesus the Saviour is his name,—
> " He freely loves, and without end."

" The words went right to the sore spot in
Clary's heart—the spot which had ached for
many a long day. Somebody to love her,—a rich

friend;—if she had written down her own wishes, they could hardly have been more perfectly expressed; and the tears came so fast, that she had to move away lest they should blot the paper. Bitter tears they were, yet not such as she had often shed; for, she knew not how, those words seemed to carry a possible hope of fulfilment—a half-promise—which her own imaginations had never done. And the first line suited her so exactly,—

' Poor, weak, and worthless.'

" ' I am all that,' thought Clary, ' but if this rich friend loves one poor person he might another. ' Jesus, the Saviour'—that must be the same that the other verse speaks of. ' *How happy are they who the Saviour obey*—' O I wish ,I knew how—I would do anything in the world to be happy! And I suppose all these rich people know all about him, and obey him, and that makes them so happy; for if he loves poor people he must love the rich a great deal more.'

" One o'clock!

" The great clock struck, and the people came tramping back to their work, or rose up from the corners where they had been eating such dinner as they had brought. Clary had forgotten all about hers—certainly it was an easy dinner to forget—but all the afternoon as the press kept on its busy way, she lived upon those two verses which she had learned by heart.

" She had no chance to read more when they left off work at night; but all the way home she scarce saw either rich or poor for the intentness with which her mind studied those words, and the hope and determination with which she resolved to find out of whom they spoke. She almost felt as if she had found him already—it seemed as if she was less friendless than she had been in the morning ; and though once and again the remembered words filled her eyes with tears, any one who knew Clary would have wondered at the step with which she went home."

" Where did she read those words ?" said Carl, who had listened with deep attention.

" On my 272d page," replied the hymn book. " For it so happened that I was printing that very day."

Carl turned to the 272d page and read the words, and then shutting the hymn book desired him to go on with his story.

" 'What made you so early, Clary?' said her mother, who had got home first.

" 'Early is it?' said Clary, when she could get

breath to speak—for she had run up all the three
pair of stairs to their little room. 'It's the same
time as always, mother — only maybe I walked
fast.   O mother! I've had such a happy day!'

"'A happy day!' said her mother, looking up
in amazement at the life of her voice and face
that were wont to be so dull and listless.   'Well
child—I'm glad on't,—you never had many.'

"'Such a happy day!' repeated Clary.   'O
mother—I read such beautiful words at the printing-office!'

"'Did you fetch the soap I wanted?' inquired
her mother.

"No — Clary had forgotten it.

"'Well don't be so happy' to-morrow that
you'll forget it,' said her mother.   'Every living
child here's as dirty as a pig, and no way of making 'em cleaner.   Tidy up the room a little, can't
you, Clary?—I've stood up on my two feet all
day.'

"So had Clary, and some nights she would
have said as much; but now that new half hope
of being happy — that new desire of doing all that
anybody could want her to do (she didn't know
why), gave her two feet new strength; and she
not only 'tidied up' the room, but even found a
little end of soap to tidy up the children withal;

and then gave them their supper and put them to bed with far less noise and confusion than usual.

"Her mother was already seated by the one tallow candle, making coarse shirts and overalls for a wholesale dealer; and Clary having at last found her thimble in the pocket of the smallest pair of trousers, sat down to work too. Never had her fingers moved so fast.

"'Mother,' she said, after a while, 'did you ever hear anybody talk about the Saviour?'

"Her mother stared.

"'What on earth, child!' she said. 'Where have you been, and who's been putting notions in your head?'

"'Nobody,' said Clary—'and I've been nowhere,—only to the office, the same as usual. But I read some beautiful verses there, mother—at dinner-time—that they were printing off on my press; and they made me feel so—I can't tell you how. But oh mother, they told about some great rich friend of poor people—poor people like us, mother—worth nothing at all, they said; and that everybody who obeyed him was happy.'

"'You'd better not plague your head with such stuff,' said her mother. 'Nobody cares about poor folks like us. Why child, rich people wouldn't touch us with a pair of tongs! Haven't I seen 'em draw up their frocks as I went by — because mine was calico, and maybe not over clean because I couldn't buy soap and bread both? I tell you Clary, rich folks thinks the poor has no right to breathe in the same world with 'em   I don't want to long, for one.'

" ' I didn't say rich *people*,' said Clary thoughtfully, but only this one :—

> ' Poor, weak, and worthless, though I am,
>   I have a rich almighty Friend.'

O mother! I wish I had !'

" ' Come child, shut up! said her mother, but not unkindly, for something in Clary's look and tone had stirred the long deadened feeling within her. 'I tell you child we must eat, and how is your work to get done if you sit there crying in that fashion ? The candle's 'most burnt out, too, and not another scrap in the house.'

" Clary dried her tears and went on with the overalls until the candle had flickered its last; and then groped her way in the dark to the little bed she and her mother occupied by that of the five children. For sleeping all together thus, the coverings went further. Dark and miserable it was; and yet when Clary laid herself down, overtaken at last by the sleep which had pursued

her all the evening; the last thought in the poor
child's mind was of those hymns, — the word on
which her heart went to sleep was that 'name
which is above every name.'

> ' How sweet the name of Jesus sounds
> In a believer's ear!'

" To Clary's great sorrow and disappointment,
when she went next day to the printing-office,
the pile of printed paper had been removed;
and not only so, but a new set of plates given
her instead of those of the hymn book. Clary's
only comfort was to repeat over and over to herself the words she had already learned, and to
try to get at their meaning. Sometimes she
thought she would ask the foreman, who was very
pleasant and good-natured — but that was only
while he was at some other press,—whenever he
came near hers, Clary was frightened and held
her head down lest he should guess what she was
thinking of. And as week after week passed on,
she grew very weary and discouraged; yet still
clinging to those words as the last hope she had.
If she could possibly have forgotten them, she
would have been almost desperate

" The winter passed, and the spring came; and
it was pleasanter now to go down to the printing-

office in the early morning, and to walk home at
night; and she could hear other people's canaries
sing, and see the green grass and flowers in other
people's courtyards; and on Sunday as she had
no work she could sit out on the doorstep —
if there weren't too many children about — or
walk away from that miserable street into some
pleasanter one.

"She had walked about for a long time one
Sunday, watching the people that were coming
from afternoon church; and now the sun was
leaving the street and she turned to leave it too,—
taking a little cross street which she had never
been in before.

"It hardly deserved the name of street, for a
single block was all its length. The houses were
not of the largest, but they looked neat and comfortable, with their green blinds and gay curtains;
and Spring was there in her earliest dress — a
green ground, well spotted with hyacinths, snow-
drops, and crocuses. It was very quiet, too, cut
short as it was at both ends; and the Sabbath of
the great city seemed to have quitted Broadway
and established itself here.

"Upon one of the low flights of steps, Clary
saw as she approached it, sat a little girl having
a book in her hand. With a dress after the very

pattern of Spring's, a little warm shawl over her shoulders, and a little chair that was just big enough, she sat there in the warm sunshine which streamed down through a gap in the houses, turning over the leaves of her book. If you had guessed the child's name from her looks, you would have called her 'Sweet Content.'

"Clary stopped a little way off to look at her; thinking bitterly of the five children she had left playing in the dirt at home; and as she stopped, the little girl began to sing,—

> ' O how happy are they
> Who the Saviour obey,
> And have laid up their treasure above.'

"The little voice had no more than brought these words to Clary's ear, when a carriage came rolling by and the rest of the verse was lost; but in an instant Clary was at the house, and feeling as if this were the only chance she ever should have, she opened the little gate and went in.

"The child ceased singing and looked up at her in some surprise.

"'I want to know ——,' said Clary,—and then suddenly recollecting her own poor dress, and comparing it with the little picture before her, she stopped short. But the words must come—they were spoken almost before Clary herself was aware.

" ' Will you please to tell me who the Saviour is ?'

" And then blushing and frightened she could almost have run away, but something held her fast.

" The child's eyes grew more and more wondering.

" ' Come in,' she said gravely, getting up from her chair, and with some difficulty keeping the book and the little shawl in their places.

" But Clary drew back.

" ' O yes — come in,' said the child, tucking the little book under her arm, and holding out her hand to Clary. ' Please come in — mother will tell you.'

" And following her little conductor, Clary found herself the next minute in a pleasant, plain, and very neat room.

" ' Mother,' said the child opening a door into the next room, but still keeping her eye upon Clary lest she should run away.—'Mother—here's a girl who never heard about Jesus.'

" ' I don't understand thee, Eunice,' said a pleasant voice, ' but I will come.' And a most pleasant face and figure followed the voice.

" ' What did thee say, child?' she inquired. with only a glance towards Clary.

" ' Tell mother what you want,' said the child encouragingly. 'Mother, she never heard about Jesus.'

" ' Thee never heard about him, poor child,' said the lady approaching Clary. 'And how dost thou live in this world of troubles without such a Friend?'

" ' I don't know, ma'am,' said Clary, weeping. 'We are very poor, and we never had any friends; and a long time ago in the winter I read a verse at the printing-office about some one who loved poor people,—and I thought maybe he would help us if he knew about us.'

" ' He knows all about thee now,' said the good Mrs. Allen, with a look of strange wonder and pity on her pleasant face. 'Sit down here child, and I will tell thee. Didst thou never hear about God?'

" ' Yes ma'am—' said Clary, hesitatingly,—' I believe I have. Mother says 'God help us,' sometimes. But we are very poor—nobody thinks much about us.'

" ' God is the helper of the poor and the father of the fatherless,' said Mrs. Allen with a grave but gentle voice, —' thee must not doubt

"'Tell mother what you want,' said the child, encouragingly.
'Mother, she never heard about Jesus!'"—P. 224.

that. Listen.—We had all sinned against God, and his justice said that we must all be punished, —that we must be miserable in this world, and when we die must go where no one can ever be happy. But though we were all so bad, God pitied us and loved us still—yet he could not forgive us, for he is perfectly just. It was as if we owed him a great debt, and until that debt was paid we could not be his children. But we had nothing to pay.

" ' Then the Son of God came down to earth, and bore all our sins and sorrows, and died for us, and paid our great debt with his own most precious blood.

" ' This is Jesus, the Saviour.'

" ' Yes ma'am,' said Clary, whose heart had followed every word, — ' that's what the verse said,—

' Jesus the Saviour, is his name,—
He freely loves, and without end."

" She stood as if forgetting there was any one in the room ; her eyes fixed on the ground, and the quiet tears running down from them,—her hands clasped with an earnestness that shewed how eagerly her mind was taking in that ' good news ' —' peace on earth and good will toward men '— which was now preached to her for the first time

" Little Eunice looked wistfully at her mother, but neither of them spoke.

" At length Mrs. Allen came softly to Clary, and laying her hand on the bowed head, she said,

" ' Jesus is the Friend of sinners — but then they must strive to sin no more. Wilt thou do it? wilt thou love and obey the Saviour who has done so much for thee ?'

" A sunbeam shot across the girl's face as she looked up for one moment, and then bursting into tears, she said,

" ' Oh if I knew how !'

" ' Ask him and he will teach thee. Pray to Jesus whenever thou art in trouble — when thy sins are too strong for thee, and thy love to him too faint, — when thou art tired or sick or discouraged. Ask him to love thee and make thee his child — ask him to prepare a place for thee in heaven. For he hath said, '*If ye shall ask anything in my name, I will do it.*''

" Little Eunice had gone softly out of the room while her mother spoke, and now returned with a little book in her hand, which was quietly placed in Clary's, after a look of assent from her mother.

" ' That's a Bible,'—said Eunice, with a face of

great pleasure. 'And you may have it and keep
it always. I wish I had a hymn book for you too,
but I've only got this one, and my Sunday school
teacher gave it to me last Sunday. But the Bible
is the word of God, and it will tell you all about
Jesus; and every bit of it is perfectly true. O
you will love it so much!—everybody does who
loves Jesus. And won't you come and read in my
hymn book sometimes?'

" 'Yes—come very often,' said Mrs. Allen, 'and
we will talk of these things.'

" And with a heart too full to speak, Clary left
the house.

" But oh what a different walk home!

'How happy are they
Who the Saviour obey—'

" She could understand that now, for with the
simple faith of a child she believed what had
been told her, and with her whole heart received
the Friend of sinners to be her friend. Her
earnest prayer that night, her one desire, was to
be his child and servant,— to obey him then became sweet work; and thenceforth through all
Clary's life, if any one had called her poor, she
would have answered out of the little hymn book
that Eunice gave her for a Christmas present,—

'Who made my heaven secure,
   Will here all good provide:
   While Christ is rich, can I be poor?
   What can I want beside?' "

" Is that all?" said Carl when he had waited
about two minutes for more.

" That is the story of one of my leaves," said
the hymn book.

" Well, I want to hear about all the others,"
said Carl—" so tell me."

" I can't "—said the hymn book. " It would
take me six weeks."

" Were you Clary's hymn-book?" said Carl.

" No, I was the other one—that belonged to
little Eunice. But years after that, several of us
met in an old auction-room,—there I learned
some of the particulars that I have told you."

" What is an auction-room?" said Carl.

" It is a sort of intelligence-office for books,"
replied the " Collection." " There I got the si-
tuation of companion to a lady, and went on a
long sea voyage. I had nothing to do but to
comfort her, however."

" And did you do it?" said Carl.

" Yes, very often," said the hymn book. " Perhaps as much as anything else except her
Bible."

" Now, my pretty little boat," said Carl the next day, " you shall tell me your story. I will hear you before that ugly old stocking."   •

Carl was lying flat on his back on the floor, holding the boat up at arm's length over his head, looking at it, and turning it about. It was a very complete little boat.

" I shall teach you not to trust to appearances," said the boat.

" What do you mean?" said Carl.

" I mean that when you have looked at me you have got the best of me."

" That's very apt to be the way with pretty things," said the stocking.

" It isn't!" said Carl. For he had more than once known his mother call him a " pretty boy."

" However that may be," said the boat, " I can't tell a story."

" Can't tell a story!—yes, you can," said Carl. " Do it, right off."

" I haven't any to tell," said the boat. " I was once of some use in the world, but now I'm of none, except to be looked at."

" Yes, you are of use," said Carl, " for I like

you; and you can tell a story, too, if you're a mind, as well as the pine cone."

" The pine cone has had a better experience," said the boat, " and has kept good society. For me, I have always lived on the outside of things, ever since I can remember, and never knew what was going on in the world, any more than I knew what was going on inside of my old tree. All I knew was, that I carried up sap for its branches —when it came down again, or what became of it, I never saw."

" Where were you then ? " said Carl.

" On the outside of a great evergreen oak in a forest of Valencia. I was a piece of its bark. I wish I was there now. But the outer bark of those trees gets dead after a while ; and then the country-people come and cut it off and sell it out of the land."

" And were you dead and sold off ? " said Carl.

" To be sure I was. As fine a piece of cork as ever grew. I had been growing nine years since the tree was cut before."

" Well but tell me your story," said Carl.

" I tell you," said the little cork boat, " I haven't any story. There was nothing to be seen in the forest but the great shades of the kingly oaks, and the birds that revelled in the solitudes of their thick branches, and the martens, and such-like. It was fine there, though. The north winds, which the pine cone says so shake the heads of the fir-trees in his country, never trouble anything in mine. The snow never lay on the glossy leaves of my parent oak. But no Norrska lived there; or if there did, I never knew her. Nobody came near us, unless a stray peasant now and then passed through. And when I was cut down, I was packed up and shipped off to England, and shifted from hand to hand, till John Krinken took it into his head, years ago, to make a sort of cork jacket of me, with one or two of my companions; and I have been tumbling about in his possession ever since. He has done for me now. I am prettier than I ever was before, but I shall never be of any use again. I shall try the water, I suppose, again a few times for your pleasure, and then probably I shall try the fire, for the same."

"The fire! No, indeed," said Carl. "I'm not going to burn you up. I am going to see you sail this minute, since you won't do anything else. You old stocking, you may wait till I come back. I don't believe *you*'ve got much of a story."

And Carl sprang up and went forthwith to the

beach, to find a quiet bit of shallow water in some nook where it would be safe to float his cork boat. But the waves were beating pretty high that day, and the tide coming in, and, altogether there was too much commotion on the beach to suit the little ' Santa Claus,' as he had named her. So Carl discontentedly came back, and set up the little boat to dry, and turned him to the old stocking.

THE STOCKING'S STORY.

" It's too bad!" said Carl. " I've heard six stories and a little piece, and now there's nothing left but this old stocking!"

" I believe I will not tell you my story at all," said the stocking.

" But you shall," said Carl, " or else I will cut you all up into little pieces."

" Then you certainly will never hear it," said the stocking.

" Well now"—said Carl. "What a disagreeable old stocking you are. Why don't you begin at once?"

" I am tired of being always at the foot"—said the stocking;—" as one may say, at the fag end. And besides your way of speaking is not proper. I suppose you have been told as much before. This is not the way little boys used to speak when *I* was knit."

"You are only a stocking," said Carl.

"Everything that is worth speaking to at all, is worth speaking to politely," replied the stocking.

"I can't help it"—said Carl,—"you might tell me your story then. I'm sure one of my own red stockings would tell its story in a minute."

"Yes," said the grey stocking; "and the story would be, 'Lived on little Carl's foot all my life, and never saw anything.' "

"It wouldn't be true then," said Carl, "for I never wear 'em except on Sundays. Mother says she can't afford it."

"Nobody afforded it once," said the stocking. "My ancestors were not heard of until ten or eleven hundred years ago, and then they were made of leather or linen. And then people wore cloth hose; and then some time in the sixteenth century silk stockings made their appearance in England. But there was never a pair of knit woollen stockings until the year 1564."

"I say," said Carl, "do stop—will you? and go on with your story." And putting his hand down into the old stocking, he stretched it out as far as he could on his little fingers.

"You'd better amuse yourself in some other

way," said the stocking. " If my yarn should break, it will be the worse for your story."

" Well why don't you begin then?" said Carl, laying him down again.

" It's not always pleasant to recount one's misfortunes," said the stocking. "And I have come down in the world sadly. You would hardly think it, I dare say, but I did once belong to a very good family."

" So you do now," said Carl. " There never was anybody in the world better than my mother; and father's very good too."

" Yes," said the stocking again,—" Mrs. Krinken does seem to be quite a respectable sort of woman for her station in life,—very neat about her house, and I presume makes most excellent chowder But you see, where I used to live, chowder had never even been heard of. I declare," said the stocking. " I can hardly believe it myself,—I think my senses are getting blunted. I have lain in that chest so long with a string of red onions, that I have really almost forgotten what musk smells like! But my Lady Darlington always fainted away if anybody mentioned onions, so of course the old Squire never had them on the dinner table even. A fine old gentleman he was: not very tall, but as straight almost as ever; and with ruddy cheeks, and hair that was not white but silver colour. His hand shook a little some times, but his heart never—and his voice was as clear as a whistle. His step went cheerily about the house and grounds, although it was only to the music of his walking-stick; and music that was, truly, to all the poor people of the neigh bourhood. His stick was like him. He would have neither gold nor silver head to it, but it was all of good English oak,—the top finely carved into a supposed likeness of Edward the Con fessor.

"As for my lady, she was all stateliness,—very beautiful too, or had been; and the sound of her dress was like the wings of a wild bird."

"I think I shall like to hear this story," said Carl, settling himself on his box and patting his hands together once or twice.

"I dare say you will," said the stocking.—" when I tell it to you. However——Well——

"A great many years ago it was Christmas-eve at Squire Darlington's, and the squire sat alone in his wide hall. Every window was fes-tooned with ivy leaves and holly, which twisted about the old carving and drooped and hung round the silver sconces, and thence downward towards the floor. The silver hands of the sconces held tall wax candles, but they were not lit. The picture frames wore wreaths, from which the old portraits looked out gloomily enough,—not finding the adornment so becoming as they had done a century or so before; and even the Squire's high-backed chair was crowned with a bunch of holly berries. There was no danger of their being in his way, for he rarely leaned back in his chair, but sat up quite straight, with one hand on his knee and the other on the arm of the chair. On that particular evening his hand rested on me; for I and my companion stocking had been put on for the first time."

"I don't see how he could get his hand on his stocking," said Carl, "if he sat up. Look—I couldn't begin to touch mine."

"You needn't try to tell me anything about stockings," replied that article of dress somewhat contemptuously. "I know their limits as well as most people. But in those days, Master Carl, gentlemen wore what they called small-clothes— very different from your new-fangled pantaloons."

"I don't wear pantaloons," said Carl,—"I wear trousers." But the stocking did not heed the interruption.

"The small-clothes reached only to the knee —a little above or a little below—and so met the long stockings half way. Some people wore very fanciful stockings, of different colours and embroidered; but Squire Darlington's were always of grey woollen yarn, very fine and soft as you see I am, and tied above the knee with black ribbons. And his shoes were always black, with large black bows and silver buckles.

"He sat there alone in the wide hall, with one hand upon me and his eyes fixed upon the fire waiting for the arrival of the Yule Clog. For in those days, the night before Yule or Christmas the chief fire in the house was built with an immense log, which was cut and brought in with great rejoicing and ceremony, and lighted with a brand saved from the log of last year. All the servants in the house had gone out to help roll the log and swell the noise, and the fire of the day had burnt down to a mere bed of coals; and the hall was so still you could almost hear the ivy leaves rustle on the old wall outside. I don't know but the Squire did."

"What did he stay there for?" said Carl. "Was he thinking?"

"He might have been," said the stocking,— · indeed I rather think he was, for he stroked and patted me two or three times. Or he might have been listening the wind sing its Christmas song."

" Can the wind sing?" said Carl.

" Ay—and sigh too. Most of all about the time of other people's holidays. It's a wild, sigh-ing kind of a song at best—whistled and sung and sighed together,—sometimes round the house, and sometimes through a keyhole. I heard what it said that night well enough. You won't un-derstand it, but this was it:—

' Christmas again! Christmas again!
With its holly berries so bright and red.
They gleam in the wood, they grow by the lane,—
O hath not Christmas a joyful tread?

Christmas again! Christmas again!
What does it find? and what does it bring?
And what does it miss that should remain?—
O Christmas time is a wonderful thing!

Christmas again! Christmas again!
There are bright green leaves on the holly tree,—
But withered leaves fly over the plain,
And the forests are brown and bare to see.

Christmas again! Christmas again!
The snow lies light and the wind is cold.
But the wind it reacheth some hearts of pain,—
And the snow—it falleth on heads grown old.

Christmas again! Christmas again!
What kindling fires flash through the hall!
The flames may flash, but the shadows remain,—
And where do the shadows this night fall?

Christmas again! Christmas again!—
It looks through the windows—it treads the floor.
Seeking for what earth could not retain—
Watching for those who will come no more.

Christmas again! Christmas again!
Why doth not the pride of the house appear?
Where is the sound of her silken train?
And that empty chair—what doeth it here?

Christmas again! Christmas again!
With hearts as light as did ever bound;
And feet as pretty as ever were fain
To tread a measure the hall around.

Christmas again! Christmas again!—
Oh thoughts, be silent! who called for ye?
Must Christmas time be a time of pain
Because of the loved, from pain set free?

Christmas again! Christmas again!—
Once Christmas and joy came hand in hand.
The hall may its holiday look regain,—
But those empty chairs must empty stand.'

" The wind took much less time to sing the song than I have taken to tell it," said the stocking,—"a low sigh round the house and a whistle or two, told all. Then suddenly a door at the lower end of the hall flew open, and a boy sprang in, exclaiming—

" ' Grandfather, it's coming!'

" He was dressed just after the fashion of the

old Squire, only with delicate white stockings and black velvet small-clothes; while his long-flapped waistcoat was gaily flowered, and his shoes had crimson rosettes. And almost as he spoke, a side-door opened and my lady glided in, her dress rustling softly as she came; while the wind rushed in after her, and tossed and waved the feathers in her tall headdress

"Then was heard a distant murmur of shouts and laughter, and young Edric clapped his hands and then stood still to listen; and presently the whole troop of servants poured into the hall from that same door at the lower end. All were dressed in the best and gayest clothes they had,—the women wore ivy wreaths, and the men carried sprigs of holly at their buttonholes. First came a number bearing torches; then many others rolling and pulling and pushing the great log, on which one of the men, whimsically dressed, was endeavouring to keep his seat; while every other man, woman, and child about the place, crowded in after.

"Then the log was rolled into the great fire-place, and duly lighted; and everybody clapped hands and rejoiced in its red glow, and Master Edric shouted as loud as the rest.

"'Edric,' said my lady when the hall was

R

quiet once more, though not empty, for all the household were to spend Christmas eve there together,—' Edric, go take a partner and dance us a minuet.'

" And Edric walked round the hall till he came to little May Underwood, the forester's daughter; and then bringing the white stockings and the crimson rosettes close side by side together, and making her a low bow, he took her hand and led her out upon the floor.

" The Yule Clog was in a full blaze now, and the clear light shone from end to end of the hall; falling upon the bright floor and the long row of servants and retainers that were ranged around, and glossily reflected from the sharp holly leaves and its bright red berries. The old portraits did not light up much, and looked very near as gloomy as ever; but a full halo of the fireshine was about the Squire's chair, and upon my lady as she stood beside him. Two or three of the serving-men played a strange old tune upon as strange old instruments; and the forester now and then threw in a few wild notes of his bugle, that sounded through the house and aroused all the echoes : but the wind sighed outside still.

" And all this while the little dancers were going through the slow, graceful steps of their pretty dance; with the most respectful bows and courtesies, the most ceremonious presenting of hands and acceptance of the same, the most graceful and complicated turns and bends; till at last when the music suddenly struck into a quick measure, Edric presented his right hand to little May, and they danced gayly forward to where my lady stood near the Squire, and made their low reverence—first to her and then to each other. Then Edric led his little partner back to her seat and returned to his grandmother. For my lady was his grandmother, and he had no parents.

" As the Yule Clog snapped and crackled and blazed higher and higher, even so did the mirth of all in the great hall. They talked and laughed and sang and played games, and not an echo in the house could get leave to be silent.

" All of a sudden, in the midst of the fun, a little boy dressed like Robin Redbreast in a dark coat and bright red waistcoat, opened one of the hall doors; and just showing himself for a moment, he flung the door clear back and an old man entered. His hair was perfectly white, and so was his beard, which reached down to his waist. On his head was a crown of yew and ivy, and in his hand a long staff topped with holly berries; his dress was a long brown robe which fell down about his feet, and on it were sewed little spots of white cloth to represent snow. He made a low bow to the Squire and my lady, and when Robin Redbreast had discreetly closed the door so far that but a little wind could come in, he began to sing in a queer little cracked voice,—

" Oh! here come I, old Father Christmas, welcome or
        not,
" I hope old Father Christmas will never be forgot.
    " Make room, room, I say,
    " That I may lead Mince Pye this way.
    " Walk in Mince Pye, and act thy part,
    " And show the gentles thy valiant heart.'

" With that Robin opened the door again and another figure came in, dressed like a woman in a dark purple gown bordered with light brownish yellow. A large apple was fastened on top of her head, and she wore bunches of raisins at her ears instead of ear-rings ; while her necklace was of large pieces of citron strung together, and her bracelets of cloves and allspice and cinnamon. In her hand she carried a large wooden sword."

" What was that for?" said Carl, who had listened with the most intense interest.

" Why to fight off the people that wanted to make her up into real mince pie, I suppose," said the stocking. "She came into the room singing,—

"Room, room, you gallant souls, give me room to rhyme,
"I will show you some festivity this Christmas time.
"Bring me the man that bids me stand,
"Who says he'll cut me down with an audacious hand;
"I'll cut him and hew him as small as a fly,
"And see what he'll do then to make his mince pye.
　　"Walk in, St. George.'
"Oh! in come I St. George, the man of courage bold.
"With my sword and buckler I have won three crowns
　　of gold;
"I fought the fiery Dragon, and brought him to the
　　slaughter,
"I saved a beauteous Queen and a King of England's
　　daughter.
　"If thy mind is high, my mind is bold;
　"If thy blood is hot, I will make it cold.'"

"What did he want to do that for?" said Carl.

"O in the days when St. George lived," replied the stocking, "the more men a man had killed the more people thought of him; and this man was trying to make himself like St. George. He had a great pasteboard helmet on his head, with a long peacock's feather streaming from the top of it, and a wooden sword, and a tin-covered shield on which were nailed clusters of holly berries in the figure of a cross. His shoes were of wood too, and his jacket and small-clothes of

buckskin, with sprigs of yew fastened down all
the seams, and great knots of red and green
ribbons at the knees. As soon as he had sung
his song he began the fight with Mince Pye,
and a dreadful fight it was, if one might judge
by the noise; also Mince Pye's sword became
quite red with the holly berries. But St. George
let his shield take all the blows, and when
Mince Pye had spent her strength upon it,
he thrust at her with his sword and down she
came."

"Who? Mince Pye?" said Carl. "Oh that's
too bad!"

"Mince Pye thought so too," said the stocking,
"for she cried out,—

"Oh! St. George, spare my life"—

"Then said old Father Christmas,—

"Is no Doctor to be found
"To cure Mince Pye, who is bleeding on the ground?"

"Was there any?" said Carl.

"There was somebody who called himself one.
He came running right into the hall the minute
old Father Christmas called for him, and you
never saw such a queer little figure. He had an
old black robe, and a black cap on his head, and a
black patch over one eye."

" What was that for?" said Carl.

" He had been curing himself, I suppose,"
said the stocking. " And it would seem that he
wasn't satisfied with any of his features, for he
had put on a long pasteboard nose painted red,
and a pointed pasteboard chin. In his hand he
carried a great basket of bottles. If one might
believe his own account, he was a doctor worth
having :—

" Oh ! yes, there is a doctor to be found
" To cure Mince Pye, who is bleeding on the ground.
" I cure the sick of every pain,
" And none of them are ever sick again."

" Father Christmas thought it must cost a
good deal to be cured after that fashion, so
like a prudent man he said,—

" Doctor, what is thy fee?"

"And the Doctor probably didn't like to be
questioned, for he answered,—

" Ten pounds is my fee;
" But fifteen I must take of thee
" Before I set this gallant free."

" But as it was necessary that Mince Pye
should be cured, Father Christmas only said,—

" Work thy will, Doctor."

" Then the Doctor took a bottle out of his basket, and began to dance and sing round Mince Pye,—

> " I have a little bottle by my side,
> " The fame of which spreads far and wide;
> " Drop a drop on this poor man's nose."

" And with that Mince Pye jumped up as well as ever."

" But that wasn't all?" said Carl. " What else ?"

" That was not quite all," said the stocking, " for another man came in, with a great basket of dolls at his back and a tall red cap on his head. And he sang, too,—

> " Oh ! in come I, little saucy Jack,
> " With all my family at my back ;
> " Christmas comes but once a-year,
> " And when it does it brings good cheer,
> " Roast beef, plum pudding, and Mince Pye—
> " Who likes that any better than I ?
> " Christmas makes us dance and sing ;
> " Money in the purse is a very fine thing.
> " Ladies and gentlemen, give us what you please.'

" Then Squire Darlington and my lady each took out some money, and Edric carried it to the masquers, and as he hadn't any money himself he told them that he was very much obliged to them ; then they went off."

" What did they give them money for ?" said Carl.

" O they expected it — that was what they came for. People used to go about in that way to the rich houses at Christmas time, to get a little money by amusing the gentlefolks."

" I s'pose they were very much amused," said Carl with a little sigh.

" Very much — especially Edric. And after they were gone he came and stood before the great fire and thought it all over, smiling to himself with pleasure.

" 'Edric,' said my lady, 'it is time for you to go to bed.'

" 'Yes grandmother—but I'm afraid I can't go to sleep.'

" 'Why not ?' said Squire Darlington. 'What are you smiling at ?'

" 'O we've had such a splendid time, grandfather !—the people were dressed so finely — and didn't Mince Pye fight well ? and wasn't the Doctor queer ! And I'm sure my stocking will be as full as *anything*.'

" Squire Darlington drew the boy towards him, and seated him on his knee while he spoke thus ;

and passing his hand caressingly over the young joyous head, and smoothing down the brown hair that was parted—child fashion—over the middle of the forehead, and came curling down upon the lace frill, he looked into Edric's face with a world of pleasure and sympathy.

" ' And so you've enjoyed the evening, dear boy ?' he said.

" ' O yes ! grandfather — so much ! I'm sure Christmas is the very happiest time of the whole year !'

" Squire Darlington stroked down the hair again, and looked in the bright eyes, but with something of wistfulness now ; and without stirring his hand from the boy's head, his look went towards the fire.

" The Yule Clog was blazing there steadily, although it now shewed a great front of glowing coals that yet had not fallen from their place. A clear red heat was all that part of the log, and hardly to be distinguished from the bed of coals below ; while bright points of flame curled and danced and ran scampering up the chimney, as if they were playing Christmas games. But each end of the log yet held out against the fire, and had not even lost its native brown.

" The Squire looked there with an earnest gaze

that was not daunted by the glowing light; but his brows were slightly raised, and though the caressing movement of his hand was repeated, it seemed now to keep time to sorrowful music; and his lips had met on that boundary line between smiles and tears. Presently a little hand was laid against his cheek, and a little lace ruffle brushed lightly over its furrows.

" 'Grandfather, what's the matter? What makes you look grave?'

" The Squire looked at him, and taking the hand in his own patted it softly against his face.

" 'The matter? my dear,' he said. 'Why the matter is that Christmas has come and gone a great many times.'

" 'But that's good, grandfather,' said Edric, clapping his hands together. 'Just think! there'll be another Christmas in a year, only a year, and we had one only a year ago—and such a nice time!'

" 'Only a year'— repeated the old man slowly. 'No Edric, it is only sixty years.'

" 'What do you mean, grandfather?' said the boy softly.

" 'Sixty years ago, my dear,' said Squire Darlington, 'there was just such a Yule Clog as that burning in this very fire-place. And the windows, and picture frames—there were not quite so many then—were trimmed with holly berries and yew from the same trees from which these wreaths have come to-day. And this old chair stood here, and everything in this old hall looked just as it does now.'

" ' Well, grandfather ?' said Edric catching his breath a little,—and the wind gave one of its lone sighs through the keyhole.

" ' Well my dear—Instead of one dear little couple on the floor '—and the old man drew the boy closer to him—' there were six,—as merry-eyed and light-footed little beings as ever trod this green earth. At the head I stood with your grandmother, Edric—a dear little thing she was !' said Squire Darlington with a kindly look to-wards my lady, whose eyes were cast down now for a wonder, and her lips trembling a little. ' Her two brothers and my two, and the orphan boy that we loved like a brother ; his sister, and my four little sisters—precious children ! that they were—made up the rest. Light feet, and soft voices, and sweet laughter—they went through this old hall like a troop of fairies, I was going to say,—more like a ray of pure human happiness.

" ' My father sat here, and my mother opposite —her picture watches the very spot now ; and of these good friends at the other end of the hall—

Ay! old Cuthbert remembers it—there were two or three; but many others that bore their names.

" ' My child—that is sixty years ago.'

" ' And where are they now, grandfather?' said Edric under his breath.

" ' In heaven—the most of them,' said the old man solemnly. 'But one couple remains of the six.—Of those other dear children not one is left —and not one but gave good hope in his death that he was going to be with Jesus. They remember yet that he came to earth. but they sing another song from ours—their hearts swell with a different joy. We shall know, one day—if we are faithful. They are exceeding fair to my remembrance,—they are fairer now in reality.'

" The old Squire was silent for a few minutes, with his eyes turned again towards the fire, while Edric looked up at the sweet portrait to which his grandfather had referred, and wondered how it was that those eyes always met his. Then Squire Darlington spoke again, and with a different manner.

" ' Everybody that has money makes Christmas a time of feasting and rejoicing, Edric,' he said. 'What does Christmas day celebrate?'

" ' The birth of Christ.' said Edric gravely.

" ' Yes '—said Squire Darlington. ' The birth of Christ. 'Who though he was rich, yet for our sakes became poor; that we through his poverty might be made rich.' There is a motto for Christmas-day!—ay—for one's whole life.'

" ' Grandfather,' said Edric, ' does everybody that loves Christ love all the poor disagreeable people?'

" ' This is what the Bible says, Edric. 'For if any man seeth that his brother have need, and shutteth up his bowels of compassion from him, how dwelleth the love of Christ in him?' '

" ' Grandfather,' said Edric thoughtfully, ' when I am a man I will take a great deal of care of poor people.'

" It was rather a sad smile that the old man gave him, and yet it was very tender.

" ' My dear Edric,' he said, ' never say, *when I am a man* I will do good. There is hardly any kind of good work that a child may not help forward, or help to keep back. Will you wait till you are a man, Edric, before you begin to love Christ?'

" ' I think I do love him now, grandfather,' said Edric. ' I should think everybody would— he has done so much for us.'

" There was the same look of love and sadness for a moment in the old man's face before he answered.

" 'My motto has another bearing, dear boy, and one which should be first in the heart of every man and every child in this world which Christ died to save,—' *If ye love me*, keep my commandments.' '

" And when the Christmas eve was almost ended, Squire Darlington kissed and blessed his little grandson, and Edric went up-stairs to bed.

" And the wind sighed no more that night."

" And did he do as he said he would, when he got to be a man?" inquired Carl

" I don't know"—said the stocking: " I never heard."

THE END OF THE STOCKING.

PRINTED BY BALLANTYNE, HANSON AND CO.
EDINBURGH AND LONDON

BOOKS

SUITABLE FOR

PRESENTS, AND FOR THE YOUNG.

PRICE EIGHTEENPENCE.

Uniform in size and binding, 16mo, Illustrations, cloth.

1. AUNT EDITH; or, Love to God the Best Motive.
2. SUSY'S SACRIFICE. By the Author of "Nettie's Mission.
3. KENNETH FORBES; or, Fourteen Ways of Studying the Bible.
4. LILIES OF THE VALLEY, and other Tales.
5. CLARA STANLEY; or, A Summer among the Hills.
6. THE CHILDREN OF BLACKBERRY HOLLOW.
7. HERBERT PERCY; or, From Christmas to Easter.
8. PASSING CLOUDS; or, Love Conquering Evil.
9. DAYBREAK; or, Right Struggling and Triumphant.
10. WARFARE AND WORK; or, Life's Progress.
11. EVELYN GREY. By the Author of "Clara Stanley.
12. THE HISTORY OF THE GRAVELYN FAMILY.
13. DONALD FRASER.
14. THE SAFE COMPASS, AND HOW IT POINTS. By the Rev. R. NEWTON, D.D.
15. THE KING'S HIGHWAY; or, Illustrations of the Commandments. By the same.
16. BESSIE AT THE SEASIDE. By JOANNA H. MATTHEWS.
17. CASPER. By the Author of "The Wide Wide World," &c.
18. KARL KRINKEN; or, The Christmas Stocking. By the same.
19. MR RUTHERFORD'S CHILDREN. By the same.
20. SYBIL AND CHRYSSA. By the same.
21. HARD MAPLE. By the same.
22. OUR SCHOOL DAYS. By C. S. H.
23. AUNT MILDRED'S LEGACY. By the Author of "The Best Cheer," &c.
24. MAGGIE AND BESSIE, AND THEIR WAY TO DO GOOD. By JOANNA H. MATTHEWS.

No. 4.

S

THE GOLDEN LADDER SERIES.

Uniform in size and binding, with Coloured Illustrations.
Crown 8vo, cloth.

1. THE GOLDEN LADDER: Stories Illustrative of the Eight Beatitudes. By SUSAN and ANNA WARNER. 3s. 6d.
2. THE WIDE WIDE WORLD. By SUSAN WARNER. 3s. 6d.
8. QUEECHY. By the same. 3s. 6d.
4. MELBOURNE HOUSE. By the same. 3s. 6d.
5. DAISY. By the same. 3s. 6d.
6. THE OLD HELMET. By the same. 3s. 6d.
7. THE THREE LITTLE SPADES. By the same. 2s. 6d.
8. NETTIE'S MISSION: Stories Illustrative of the Lord's Prayer. By ALICE GRAY. 3s. 6d.
9. DAISY IN THE FIELD. By SUSAN WARNER. 3s. 6d.
10. STEPPING HEAVENWARD. By Mrs PRENTISS, Author of "Little Susy's Six Birthdays." 2s. 6d.
11. WHAT SHE COULD. By the Author of "The Wide Wide World," &c. 3s. 6d.
12. GLEN LUNA; or, Dollars and Cents. By ANNA WARNER, Author of "The Golden Ladder." 3s. 6d.
13. DRAYTON HALL. Tales Illustrative of the Beatitudes. By ALICE GRAY. 3s. 6d.
14. WITHIN AND WITHOUT. 3s. 6d.
15. STORIES OF VINEGAR HILL. Illustrative of the Parable of the Sower. By A. WARNER. 3s. 6d.
16. LITTLE SUNBEAMS. Stories by JOANNA MATTHEWS. 3s. 6d.
17. TRADING, AND THE HOUSE IN TOWN. In One Volume. 3s. 6d.
18. GIVING HONOUR: Containing "The Little Camp on Eagle Hill," and "Willow Brook." By the Author of "The Wide Wide World," &c. 3s. 6d.
19. DARE TO DO RIGHT. By the Author of "Nettie's Mission." 3s. 6d.
20. SCEPTRES AND CROWNS, AND THE FLAG OF TRUCE. By the Author of "The Wide, Wide World." 3s. 6d.
21. URBANÉ AND HIS FRIENDS. By the Author of "Stepping Heavenward." 2s. 6d.
22. HOLDEN WITH THE CORDS. By the Author of "Without and Within." 3s. 6d.
23. GIVING TRUST: Containing "Bread and Oranges," and "The Rapids of Niagara." Tales Illustrating the Lord's Prayer. By SUSAN WARNER. 3s. 6d. (Copyright.)

PRICE ONE SHILLING.

Uniform in size and binding, 16mo, Illustrations, each 1s. cloth.

1. CHANGES UPON CHURCH BELLS. By C. S. H.
2. GONZALEZ AND HIS WAKING DREAMS. By C. S. H.
3. DAISY BRIGHT. By EMMA MARSHALL.
4. HELEN; or, Temper and its Consequences. By Mrs G. GLADSTONE.
5. THE CAPTAIN'S STORY; or, The Disobedient Son. By W. S. MARTIN.
6. THE LITTLE PEATCUTTERS; or, The Song of Love. By EMMA MARSHALL.
7. LITTLE CROWNS, AND HOW TO WIN THEM. By the Rev. J. A. COLLIER.
8. CHINA AND ITS PEOPLE. By a MISSIONARY'S WIFE.
9. TEDDY'S DREAM; or, A Little Sweep's Mission.
10. ELDER PARK; or, Scenes in our Garden. By Mrs ALFRED PAYNE, Author of "Nature's Wonders," &c.
11. HOME LIFE AT GREYSTONE LODGE. By the Author of "Agnes Falconer."
12. THE PEMBERTON FAMILY, and other Stories.
13. CHRISTMAS AT SUNBERRY DALE. By W. B. B.
14. PRIMROSE; or, The Bells of Old Effingham.
15. THE BOY GUARDIAN. By C. E. Bowen, Author of "Dick and his Donkey."
16. VIOLET'S IDOL. By JOANNA H. MATTHEWS.
17. FRANK GORDON. By F. R. GOULDING. And LITTLE JACK'S FOUR LESSONS. By ANNA WARNER.
18. THE COTTAGE BY THE CREEK. By the Hon. Mrs CLIFFORD-BUTLER.
19. THE WILD BELLS, AND WHAT THEY RANG.
20. TO-DAY AND YESTERDAY. A Story of Summer and Winter Holidays.
21. GLASTONBURY; or, The Early British Christians. By Mrs ALFRED PAYNE.
22. MAX: A Story of the Oberstein Forest.
23. LUPICINE; or, The Hermit of St Loup.
24. MARY TRELAWNY. A Story for Little Girls.
25. LOVING-KINDNESS; or, The Ashdown Flower Show.
26. BETWEEN THE CLIFFS; or, Hal Forrester's Anchor. By Mrs MARSHALL.
27. FRITZ; or, The Struggles of a Young Life. By the Author of "Max."

SELECT SERIES

All uniform, crown 8vo, 3s. 6d. cloth.

1. DERRY. A Tale of the Revolution. By CHARLOTTE ELIZABETH.

2. THE LAND OF THE FORUM AND THE VATICAN. By NEWMAN HALL, LL.B.

3. THE LISTENER. By CAROLINE FRY.

4. DAYS AND NIGHTS IN THE EAST; or, Illustrations of Bible Scenes. By HORATIUS BONAR, D.D. Illustrations.

5. THE HOLY WAR. By JOHN BUNYAN. Coloured Illustrations.

6. THE PILGRIM'S PROGRESS. By JOHN BUNYAN. Coloured Illustrations.

7. THE MOUNTAINS OF THE BIBLE: Their Scenes and their Lessons. By the Rev. JOHN MACFARLANE, LL.D.

8. HOME AND FOREIGN SERVICE; or, Pictures in Active Christian Life.

9. LIFE: A Series of Illustrations of the Divine Wisdom in the Forms, Structures, and Instincts of Animals. By P. H. GOSSE, F.R.S.

10. LAND AND SEA. By P. H. GOSSE, F.R.S.

11. JOHN KNOX AND HIS TIMES. By the Author of "The Story of Martin Luther."

12. HOME IN THE HOLY LAND. By Mrs FINN.

13. A THIRD YEAR IN JERUSALEM. A Tale illustrating Incidents and Customs in Modern Jerusalem. By the same.

14 and 15. THE ROMANCE OF NATURAL HISTORY. By P. H. GOSSE, F.R.S. First and Second Series.

16. BLOOMFIELD. A Tale. By ELIZABETH WARREN, Author of "John Knox and his Times," &c.

17. TALES FROM ALSACE; or, Scenes and Portraits from Life in the Days of the Reformation, as Drawn from Old Chronicles. Translated from the German.

18. HYMNS OF THE CHURCH MILITANT. Edited by the Author of "The Wide Wide World," &c.

19. THE PHYSICIAN'S DAUGHTERS; or, The Spring-Time of Woman.

20. WANDERING HOMES AND THEIR INFLUENCES. By the Author of "The Physician's Daughters."

21. THE INGLISES; or, How the Way Opened. By the Author of "Christie Redfern's Troubles."

22. LOWENCESTER. A Tale. By SYDNEY HAMPDEN.

BOOKS FOR THE YOUNG

BY THE REV. J. R. MACDUFF, D.D.

1. FOOTSTEPS OF ST PAUL. Being a Life of the Apostle. Designed for Youth. With Illustrations. Thirty-first Thousand, crown 8vo, 5s. cloth.

2. TALES OF THE WARRIOR JUDGES. A Sunday Book for Boys. Third Thousand. Fcap. 8vo, 2s. 6d. cloth.

3. THE STORY OF BETHLEHEM. With Illustrations by THOMAS. Eighth Thousand, crown 8vo, 2s. 6d. cloth.

4. THE EXILES OF LUCERNA; or, The Sufferings of the Waldenses during the Persecution of 1866. Fourth Thousand, 16mo, 2s. 6d. cloth.

5. THE WOODCUTTER OF LEBANON. Seventh Thousand, 16mo, 2s. cloth.

6. THE GREAT JOURNEY: A Pilgrimage through the Valley of Tears to Mount Zion, the City of the Living God. Sixth Thousand, 16mo, 1s. 6d. cloth.

7. THE CITIES OF REFUGE; or, The Name of Jesus. A Sunday Book. Tenth Thousand, 16mo, 1s. 6d. cloth.

8. THE LITTLE CHILD'S BOOK OF DIVINITY; or, Grandmamma's Stories about Bible Doctrines. Thirteenth Thousand, 16mo, 1s. cloth limp.

9. WILLOWS BY THE WATERCOURSES; or, God's Promises to the Young. A Text Book. Eighth Thousand, 64mo, 3d. sewed, 6d. cloth limp.

10. FERGUS MORTON; or, The Story of a Scottish Boy. 16mo, 9d. cloth.

BALLANTYNE'S MISCELLANY

OF ENTERTAINING AND INSTRUCTIVE TALES.

16mo, Illustrations, 1s. each, cloth.

Or, in sets, with handsome cloth box, price 17s. 6d.

---

1. FIGHTING THE WHALES; or, Doings and Dangers on a Fishing Cruise.
2. AWAY IN THE WILDERNESS; or, Life among the Red Indians and Fur Traders of North America.
3. FAST IN THE ICE; or, Adventures in the Polar Regions.
4. CHASING THE SUN; or, Rambles in Norway.
5. SUNK AT SEA; or, The Adventures of Wandering Will in the Pacific.
6. LOST IN THE FOREST; or, Wandering Will in South America.
7. OVER THE ROCKY MOUNTAINS; or, Wandering Will in the Land of the Redskin.
8. SAVED BY THE LIFE-BOAT; or, A Tale of Wreck and Rescue on the Coast.
9. THE CANNIBAL ISLANDS or, Captain Cook's Adventures in the South Seas.
10. HUNTING THE LIONS; or, The Land of the Negro.
11. DIGGING FOR GOLD; or, Adventures in California.
12. UP IN THE CLOUDS; or, Balloon Voyages.
13. THE BATTLE AND THE BREEZE; or, The Fights and Fancies of a British Tar.
14. THE PIONEERS: A Tale of the Western Wilderness.
15. THE STORY OF THE ROCK.
16. WRECKED BUT NOT RUINED.

WORKS BY R. M. BALLANTYNE.

Crown 8vo, with Illustrations, each 5s. cloth,

RIVERS OF ICE:
A TALE ILLUSTRATIVE OF ALPINE ADVENTURE AND GLACIER ACTION.

THE PIRATE CITY:
AN ALGERINE TALE.

BLACK IVORY:
A TALE OF ADVENTURE AMONG THE SLAVERS OF EAST AFRICA.

THE NORSEMEN IN THE WEST;
OR, AMERICA BEFORE COLUMBUS.

THE FLOATING LIGHT OF THE GOODWIN SANDS.

THE GOLDEN DREAM:
A TALE OF THE DIGGINGS.

ERLING THE BOLD:
A TALE OF THE NORSE SEA-KINGS.

DEEP DOWN: A TALE OF THE CORNISH MINES.

FIGHTING THE FLAMES:
A TALE OF THE LONDON FIRE-BRIGADE.

SHIFTING WINDS: A TOUGH YARN.

THE LIGHTHOUSE;
OR, THE STORY OF A GREAT FIGHT BETWEEN MAN AND THE SEA.

THE LIFEBOAT:
A TALE OF OUR COAST HEROES.

GASCOYNE, THE SANDALWOOD TRADER:
A TALE OF THE PACIFIC.

THE IRON HORSE; OR, LIFE ON THE LINE.

LONDON: JAMES NISBET & CO., 21 BERNERS STREET.